"Police!"

I cursed under my breath and felt around in the darkness for my table lamp, found it, and checked the small travel clock on the end table. Three o'clock. Nothing good ever happens at three o'clock in the friggin' morning.

"Paul, don't get near the door!"

Mommy wisdom. Just before Christmas, somebody had shot through a door on the floor above us. I stood to one side, pulling on my jeans.

"What you want?" I called, trying to sound older than sixteen.

"Richard DuPree live here?"

"No."

"He's been hurt."

I looked through the peephole. Two cops. I opened the door.

I've Seen the Promised Land: The Life of Dr. Martin Luther King, Jr.
Illustrated by Leonard Jenkins

Shooter

The Dream Bearer

Handbook for Boys: A Novel

Patrol: An American Soldier in Vietnam
Illustrated by Ann Grifalconi

Bad Boy: A Memoir

Malcolm X: A Fire Burning Brightly
Illustrated by Leonard Jenkins

Monster

Angel to Angel: A Mother's Gift of Love

Glorious Angels: A Celebration of Children

The Story of the Three Kingdoms
Illustrated by Ashley Bryan

Brown Angels: An Album of Pictures and Verse

The Righteous Revenge of Artemis Bonner

Now Is Your Time!: The African-American Struggle for Freedom

The Mouse Rap

Scorpions

Tales of a Dead King

ALL THE RIGHT STUFF

by

WALTER DEAN MYERS

Amistad

An Imprint of HarperCollinsPublishers

Amistad is an imprint of HarperCollins Publishers.

All the Right Stuff
Copyright © 2012 by Walter Dean Myers

Library of Congress Cataloging-in-Publication Data
Myers, Walter Dean.
    All the right stuff / by Walter Dean Myers. — 1st ed.
        p.   cm.
    Summary: The summer after his absentee father is killed in a random
shooting, Paul works at a Harlem soup kitchen, where he listens to
lessons about "the social contract" from an elderly African American
man and mentors a seventeen-year-old unwed mother who wants to
make it to college on a basketball scholarship.
    ISBN 978-0-06-196089-5
    [1. Coming of age—Fiction.   2. Conduct of life—Fiction.   3. Social
contract—Fiction.   4. African Americans—Fiction.   5. Harlem (New
York, NY)—Fiction.   I. Title.
PZ7.M992A1 2012   2011024251
[Fic]—dc22   CIP
                                                                           AC

Typography by Michelle Gengaro-Kokmen
13 14 15 16 17   LP/RRDH   10 9 8 7 6 5 4 3 2 1
❖
First paperback edition, 2013

My thanks to Peter Minowitz,
professor of political science, Santa Clara University,
for his careful reading and valuable insights

To live is not merely to breathe: It is to act; it is to make use of our organs, senses, faculties—of all those parts of ourselves which give us the feeling of existence.

—Jean-Jacques Rousseau

There are two kinds of equality; that which consists in dividing the same advantages indiscriminately among all the citizens, and that which consists in distributing them to each according to his deserts.

—Isocrates

1

"Police!"

I cursed under my breath and felt around in the darkness for my table lamp, found it, and checked the small travel clock on the end table. Three o'clock. Nothing good ever happens at three o'clock in the friggin' morning.

"Paul, don't get near the door!"

Mommy wisdom. Just before Christmas, somebody had shot through a door on the floor above us. I stood to one side, pulling on my jeans.

"What you want?" I called, trying to sound older than sixteen.

"Richard DuPree live here?"

"No."

"He's been hurt."

I looked through the peephole. Two cops. I opened the door.

The officers filled the narrow space between my apartment and my next-door neighbor's. Down the hallway, I saw Mrs. Rivers poke her head out for a second, then quickly disappear.

"We come in for a moment?" The officer's voice was calm.

Mom gestured with one hand and held her robe tight with the other. On the kitchen table, a half bottle of Red Devil hot sauce stood next to a plate I had forgotten to wash.

"What happened?" Mom asked.

"There was a fight—I don't think he was directly involved in it—"

"So what happened?"

"What's your relationship with him?"

"My father, but . . . he doesn't live with us," I answered.

"Your name?"

"Paul."

"Paul, I'm really sorry, but—"

Mom burst into tears before he could finish.

There were questions. Did my father have any

disagreements with anyone? Was he a street person? How long had he lived away from home?

I just wanted them to leave. We didn't have the answers they needed. We didn't want to give them the answers we had.

My dad had never really lived with us. It was more precise to say that he came around when he wasn't doing a bid. He had been out of jail nearly two years this time and was actually working. At least when I saw him, he wasn't doping himself up. He lived three blocks away in a little kitchenette that he liked to say was "just big enough to change your mind in."

The cops weren't in a hurry. They sat and talked for a half hour, telling us where we could go to get details later from the police, where my father's body was; and they gave us the number of an organization that helped crime victims. When they left, Mom went into the bathroom and threw up.

I didn't love my father. I wanted to, but I didn't. Sometimes I didn't even like him. He hadn't been a guy you could really get next to, because in a way he was never where you thought he was. If I ran into him on the street, he would try to halfway get himself together by brushing off his clothes or trying to say something he thought would make him sound smart. Nothing wrong with that except that you could see it coming and it never worked. Or maybe I just wanted something more from him?

He and Mom had had something going once, but as soon as she had gotten pregnant with me, he got scarce. I thought he might have loved Mom, but from what I could see, he never seemed to have enough of whatever it took to have a real relationship. Since he had been out the last time, he had been coming around more often. Mom was talking about how he was "settling," as she called it, and I thought they were thinking about trying to get something started again. I wasn't for it, but I wasn't against it, either. I wasn't sure if Mom actually cared for him or just needed somebody bad enough to take him back.

The funeral was held in a small private chapel on Lenox Avenue. It was hot outside, and the fans stirred the heat around the small room. I didn't recognize half of the people there. My father was dressed neatly, looking better in his coffin than he had looked walking around. Two women I recognized as his aunts—their makeup, a flat beige, looking as pale as the makeup they had put on my father's face—were making noises as if they had really been close to him. It was a struggle for Mom to even listen to them.

"Ebony, I know how you must feel, girl."

Mom was too overcome with emotion to say much of anything. I just felt kind of cheated. I should have felt sad, but somewhere deep inside, I knew I had wanted so much more from the man who lay in the front of the room. I remembered how, when I was a kid, I would think about being in danger and having him come to rescue me. In my dreams, he would come bursting through a door and I would leap up and cheer as he knocked out the bad guys. In real life, he never came.

They got the guy who shot him. A twenty-year-old dude had been arguing with a clerk in the bodega on the corner about the price of loose cigarettes. He shot through the store window to "teach the clerk some respect." Instead of hitting the window, he had hit forty-two-year-old Richard DuPree, underemployed ex-felon, ex-drug addict, father of one.

Mom cried every day. Sometimes, when she wasn't telling me that I was all she had, she was blaming herself for my father's being killed. It wasn't a thought-out thing, where she had added up the pieces and had come to a conclusion. She hadn't caused him to use drugs or steal to pay for them. It was just Mom's feeling that she could have done more for him. It saddened me to see the hurt in her come to the surface like that. I had always known somehow that she was holding on to the hurt about her and my father not being together. I didn't have any answers for her, but I promised myself that I would somehow be more than he had been. I would get myself ready to burst through doors for her. To be the hero he had never been.

My school had been notified about four community jobs at ten dollars an hour over the summer. Fifty kids applied, and four of us actually got one of them. Three were at Harlem Hospital on 135th and Lenox, and one was in a soup kitchen for senior citizens. I got the soup kitchen.

"You're lucky," Mrs. Brown, my guidance counselor at Frederick Douglass Academy, said, smiling. "You work four days in the soup kitchen and then you get to mentor for three hours on Fridays. But you get paid for the entire day."

"Who am I mentoring?" I asked.

"I don't know who," Mrs. Brown said. "I know *where*. At the Harlem School of the Arts. Nine o'clock Friday mornings. Got it?"

"Yeah."

It was cool. I really wanted to work in an office or something like that, but a soup kitchen was okay, and it was in the hood. So was the Harlem School of the Arts. So I could walk to work and save carfare.

I was late for my first day at the soup kitchen because I couldn't find the place. It wasn't marked SOUP KITCHEN or anything like that. It was on the basement floor of a brownstone on 144th Street, and there was a small sign over the bell that read ELIJAH JONES'S SOUP EMPORIUM.

I rang the bell and a small, bright-eyed man with gray hair answered. He looked old.

"My name is Paul DuPree," I said. "And I'm supposed to be working here four days a week."

"Welcome, Mr. Paul DuPree," he said. "I'm Elijah Jones. Please come in."

I followed him in, through a room with six long tables set up and into a large, airy kitchen. The sunlight shone through the back windows and lit up the place nicely. Mr. Jones sat himself down at one end of the table in the kitchen and gestured toward the other stool. I sat down.

"Hand me one of those vidalias over there, please." He pointed in my direction, then started cutting up vegetables for the soup we were making.

I looked over to where he was pointing and didn't see what he was talking about. The only things sitting on the bench were some onions.

"Some *what*?" I asked him.

He put down the knife he was chopping carrots with and turned toward me. "Give me your particulars again?"

"Paul DuPree," I said. "Sixteen years old and just finished eleventh grade."

"Did you want to add anything in there about not knowing what a vidalia was?" he asked.

"Not really," I said.

"Well, a vidalia is a sweet onion," Elijah said. "I reckon most people would know that. What do you know about onions, anyway?"

"I know I don't eat them," I said.

"I guess that's what the world is coming to today," he said, turning back to his cutting board. "We got wars going on all over the world, we got people robbing and shooting each other, and we got young people like you don't even know what a vidalia is. You thinking this might be the end of the world creeping up on us?"

"No, sir, it's more about you dealing with onions and your vegetables, Mr. Jones," I said. "And if it was the end of the world, I don't think your onions would help too much."

"You'll call me Elijah," he said. "And I rather resent your opinion of the power of onions."

"Sorry . . . Elijah," I said.

"How about the soup? You think the soup would save the world?"

My man had a soup emporium, so I figured he was definitely into soup. "If you say so," I said.

"You never heard of anybody doing anything really bad while they were having a bowl of soup," he said. "At least I haven't. You ever hear the newscaster come on and say, 'Man robs bank while eating a bowl of chicken noodle soup?' Nope. You ever see a headline that said CRAZED KILLER SHOOTS FIVE PEOPLE WHILE EATING A BOWL OF MOCK TURTLE SOUP? Nope, you have not."

Elijah told me he was eighty-four, but he didn't look like what I thought a man that old would. He was dark, maybe five six or seven, and thin but not really skinny. He stood straight as an arrow and moved around his kitchen almost as if he was dancing.

"So you're saving the world with your soup?" I asked.

"I hear the smile in your voice, Mr. DuPree," Elijah said. "And I'll let you know I'm not about saving all of it, just my little corner here in Harlem. The way my mind works is that if we could get everybody to save their own little piece of this planet, then eventually we'd get the whole thing in pretty good shape."

"Yes, sir."

"If I'm part of this summer grant program next year, I'm going to ask them to send me a young man who at least knows something about onions," Elijah said.

"Yes, sir."

I watched Elijah make the soup of the day and get some vegetables ready for the next day's soup. At twelve o'clock, the first people started drifting in, and he had me serve them.

The thing was that all the people knew Elijah, and they were enjoying themselves, eating the soup and talking to each other. It seemed that they weren't all that hungry so much as they were just people who liked to be together. Elijah didn't say a lot to me. Once in a while he would point to something, like a spot on a tablecloth, and I had to figure out that he meant for me to clean it up. I got the feeling that he was looking me over and seeing what I was going to bring. The day went fast in the morning, and slower in the afternoon.

For most of the afternoon, I cleaned anything that could be cleaned. Some of the things didn't even look dirty to me. This included the stove and the table and the floors. When everything was cleaned up, Elijah sat down at his cutting board, which was his favorite spot, and rolled an onion—okay, it was a vidalia—over to me.

"It's about time for you to be going now, but I want you to stop past the butcher's shop on your way here tomorrow—talk to Vinnie over there—and pick me up ten pounds of veal bones. You think you can remember that?"

"Ten pounds of veal bones," I repeated. "You going to make bone soup?"

"The best soups start with a good liquid base,"

Elijah said. "The bones are to give some body to that base. People like soup made from a good stock."

"People like any soup that's free," I said. "You're making soup and giving it away for nothing. Naturally they like it."

"I'm not just making soup," Elijah said. "I'm making good soup for the senior citizens on this block. They can come here in the afternoon if they have a mind to, sit down, and have a nice bowl of soup. It's the little pleasures in life that make it all worthwhile."

"If your soup is so good, you should charge for it," I said. "You go downtown and they have places you can buy cups of soup and they charge four or five dollars for them."

"Number one, I am not downtown," Elijah said, taking out the little purse he kept his money in. "I am Elijah I. Jones, and I am here in Harlem. If I were looking to make money, I would be charging for my soup. What I am looking to do is to bring something to the people. I have added that to my contract."

"What contract?" I asked. "You getting money from the city?"

"The social contract," Elijah said. "I know that you

understand what I'm talking about so you can see how the soup fits in."

"This is supposed to be a social club?" I asked.

"Don't pay more than five dollars for those bones," Elijah said. "And don't forget them because I'm running out of stock. And remember, the first thing I need you to do when you get here tomorrow is to stir the beans in the pot. I'm making black bean soup. Those vidalias are going into that soup."

"So what's this contract?" I said. "Who you working for?"

"The social contract?" Elijah pushed his head forward and squinted at me. "You don't know what the social contract is all about? I guess if you can't tell the difference between a vidalia onion and a regular onion, you just don't know much, do you?"

"I guess not," I said, trying not to smile.

"Just about everybody in the world is involved in some kind of social contract," Elijah said. "And that's true whether they know it or not. People think you know it, the government thinks you know it, and everybody is ready to punish you if you don't know it. Now how about that?"

"If you say so."

"If *I* say so?" Elijah put down the jar of cumin seeds he was holding and looked over at me. "Suppose I told you that if you walked down a certain street in New York, you would find hundred-dollar bills just lying on the sidewalk, ready for you to pick up. Would that interest you?"

"Sure it would."

"And suppose I told you there was another street, in the same neighborhood, where if you put one foot on the street, you would be shot on sight," Elijah said. "Now, would that interest your sixteen-year-old butt?"

"Yeah, that would interest me, too," I said. "But I never heard of either of those streets, and I know they don't exist because if they did, everybody would be talking about them."

"I can't fool you, can I?"

"Not hardly," I said.

"Mr. DuPree, the social contract is like those two streets," Elijah said. "There are rules in the contract that say you're supposed to act in a certain way and receive a certain benefit. And if you don't act the way you're supposed to, you're going to be left out of those benefits. Now, if you've already been on this planet some sixteen years and you don't know about these rules, or if you're not clear about them, you have a problem."

"I guess I have a problem," I said.

"But you don't really believe that you have a problem because you haven't heard of the social contract and I'm just an old man making soup for other old people, right?"

"I didn't say that," I answered.

"Well, Mr. DuPree, you think about it tonight and let me know what you got figured out when you get here in the morning," Elijah said.

"And take that onion with you so you two can get acquainted."

The job seemed really easy. Elijah's Soup Emporium, as he liked to call it, was just the bottom floor of a brownstone that Elijah had made into a private dining hall. There wasn't a huge sign on the place, and if you didn't see some of the seniors coming in around noon, you wouldn't know it even existed. Just inside the door, there was a coat rack, and then there was a dining room with long tables with chairs that people ate at. The kitchen was off to one side. The stove was big and modern looking with six burners. There was a large refrigerator, a freezer, a microwave, and more pots and pans than I could imagine anybody ever needing.

There was nothing much to cutting up vegetables or cleaning the kitchen or the dining room. I had never actually met anyone like Elijah before. He was smart, but not like old people are wise smart. A little bookish. He was funny, too, and that made him easy to work with. We would work in the mornings making soup, and then, between twelve and two, we would serve bowls of soup and rolls and butter to old people from the neighborhood.

Another thing that Elijah knew was history. Sometimes he would go off on a lecture about how they ran the civil service system in ancient China or how India and Pakistan used to be one country. It was not stuff I needed to know about, but it was interesting. I got the feeling he liked me, even when he was kidding me about not knowing about some vegetable.

"Did you know that garlic and onions are all varieties of lilies?" he asked me.

"No, I didn't know that," I said.

"And you still haven't figured out what the social contract is?"

"No, sir," I said. "I haven't."

When I got home, I asked my mom what she knew about some social contract.

"I know what a contract is, and I know what being social is," she said. "But I've never heard of being sociable by no contract unless you're a hooker or something."

She went on asking me what I had done that day and I told her about getting the stuff ready for the next day's soup and she said that was good. "A man who can cook can find a wife easier than a man who can't," she said.

I didn't want a wife who wanted me for my cooking, but I didn't say that to Mom.

2

When I arrived in the morning, Elijah was already up and being busy around the huge black stove.

"So I guess you got the social contract all figured out," he said to me. "Why don't you explain it to me while you wash your hands? Wash them all the way up to the elbows, too, like you're getting ready for surgery. We don't serve any dirt around here."

"I still don't get it," I said. "It seems to me that if anything really big was going on, I would have heard about it."

"You've heard about it," Elijah said. "You just didn't know how to call it by its right name."

"If you say so," I said.

I watched Elijah take a bag from the refrigerator, open it, and carefully lay out a pile of bones. He held them up and inspected them, nodded to himself, and then brought out a roasting pan. He put the bones in the pan, poured two cups of water over them, and put them into the oven. He turned the oven on and then turned back to me.

"The first thing you have to know about the social contract is what I call the wake-up-in-the-morning laws," he said. "When you wake up in the morning, you begin thinking about what you can do with yourself during the day. What's the first thing you think about doing, Mr. DuPree?"

"Depends on how I feel that morning," I said.

"There you go," Elijah said. "I was telling people that you were a smart young man. Humans can do anything they want. If you feel like eating a ham sandwich, then you go on and eat a ham sandwich. If you don't have a ham sandwich and you see I got one, then you come over to where I am, hit me on the head, and take my sandwich. That's because as a human being you can do *what*?"

"Anything I want," I said.

"Now, isn't that good?"

"Yeah, but . . . I don't go around hitting people on the head," I said. "The way you put it—you know, people doing anything they want—there would be a lot of fighting going on."

"But the possibility of doing anything you want is the key to the social contract," Elijah said. "You don't have to do geometry or algebra to figure that out. You just sit down and use your reason, and *bam!* you got it. But, like you said, there's going to be a whole lot of fighting going on. So how would Mr. DuPree handle that?"

"You keep your hands off my ham sandwich, and I'll keep my hands off your ham sandwich," I said.

"So what you're saying is that you have the right to do anything you want, but you'll give up some of your rights if I give up some of mine?" Elijah asked.

"Okay, I'll go for that," I said.

"Are we just talking about ham sandwiches here, boy?" Elijah asked me.

I looked at Elijah to see if he was making fun of me, but he looked serious. "I don't know exactly what we are talking about," I said. "You were the one who brought up the ham sandwich."

"What we're talking about is the right of a person to do anything they want to do, and comparing it with the decision to give up some of those rights so everybody can get along without a lot of fighting," Elijah said. "I'm willing to give up my right to knock you in your head and take your ham sandwich if you're willing to give up your right to hit me and take mine. That sound good to you?"

"Yeah."

"So my giving up some of my natural rights in exchange for you doing likewise is an agreement we're making," Elijah said. "You still with me, or you getting a headache?"

"I got you covered," I said.

"Well, Mr. Paul DuPree, that agreement is at the heart of the social contract we've been talking about. You are giving up your natural liberty and taking on a different kind of liberty. What you're gaining is what the first writers of the social contract called a civil liberty, the liberty to do anything you and all the other people who are part of your social contract have decided as a group to allow. People have been making agreements about what rights they are going to give up so they can live together, be safe, and chase after whatever little dreams they have going for themselves. That's been going on since they lived in caves umpteen thousand years ago."

"I never heard of no cavemen drawing up con-tracts," I said. "You ever see those drawings they find in caves? They have pictures of animals or hunting scenes, but I've never heard of any contracts."

"Okay, Mr. DuPree, if the cavemen didn't have written-out contracts, they still had rules that you had to live by if you were going to stay in the tribe," he said. "And if you didn't live by those rules, they wouldn't have any trouble kicking you out, and every-body would understand why. Those rules came by agreement, and they were part of the first social con-tracts."

"No offense, sir, but are you saying I'm supposed to care about what some cavemen were doing?" I asked. "Because I don't."

"Don't care a bit!" Elijah said, shaking his head.

"Yo, I see how you care and everything, and I respect that," I said. "You know, different strokes for different folks. I just mean that it really doesn't get to a point where I can feel it."

"I care about it, Mr. DuPree, because I believe that the tribes with the best rules were the ones that survived!" Elijah said. "And that seems important to me. If you play one of those video games in which there are warriors running around trying to kill each other, you understand that survival is important."

"You play video games?" I asked.

"I've played a few," Elijah answered. "And the few I've played had rules to help you survive. And if you're going to play those games, you have to agree to live by the rules. Or do you have a different kind of game, Mr. DuPree?"

"Okay, I see where you're coming from but—I mean this truly—we don't need agreements and contracts and whatnot today because we have laws," I said.

"You really think that's true?" Elijah asked. "Look me right in the face and say it again, real slow."

"I said, we don't need those rules because we have laws," I said. "Laws replace rules."

"Sit down right there and start slicing up some of those onions while I talk to you, son," Elijah said. "And please don't cut your fingers up into the onions, because blood makes the soup salty."

I sat down and started cutting the onions as he watched me. He let me cut two onions before he started talking again.

"We don't have a law that says a man needs to get out and find himself a job, do we?" Elijah asked.

He held his hand up before I could speak.

"And if he does have a job and wants to spend his money on beer and lottery tickets on the way home from work and not feed his family, that's not illegal, is it?"

The hand went up again, and I kept quiet.

"There's a law that says you have to go to school, but there's no law that says you have to learn anything. If you get on the crosstown bus and you want to stick your tongue out at everybody on the bus, you can do it and you're as legal as the day is long, am I right?"

"Can I answer?"

"You got a mouth, use it," Elijah said.

"It's legal, but I don't want to stick my tongue out at everybody on the bus," I said.

"Okay, but how many people you see won't shake a stick at a piece of work?" Elijah asked. "And how many you see down at the bar or wherever they go spending their money instead of taking care of their families? You see any of that around where you live?"

"Plenty," I said.

"And how many young people—and old people, too—do you hear cursing on that bus we're talking about?"

"I guess a few," I said.

"And how many young people you see walking out that little delicatessen on the corner—"

"The one next to the barber shop?" I asked.

"That's the one," Elijah said. "They come out eating their fruity pops or their poppy fruits or whatever young people cram into their mouths today, and throw the wrappers on the ground. Can I get an amen on that?"

"Amen."

"But what you want to tell me is that those things aren't that important, right?" Elijah had folded his arms across his chest. "A candy wrapper don't mean anything even if it is lying on the sidewalk, and if a man wants to spend his money down at the bar instead of bringing it on home to his family . . . well, that's his right. Isn't that what you want to tell Elijah?"

"It's important to you," I said. "I can see that."

"Would we be living better or worse if that man we talking about had a job and if the young person throwing their fruity pops wrapper on the ground put it in the trash can?"

"I wouldn't be living any different," I said. "If the guy didn't feed his family, that's his business."

"And that's his right under that first wake-up-in-the-morning law," Elijah said. "But if you have to pay taxes to feed his family, then what's going on?"

"I didn't think about that," I said.

"And if you have to pay taxes to get somebody to go around picking up fruity pops wrappers, then that's all right with you, too?"

"I didn't say that it was all right," I said.

"And suppose I told you that there are unwritten contracts in our society that say that if you don't follow them, you're going to suffer all your life?" he went on. "Take that little business about going to school. You sitting up in school daydreaming about your career in the National Basketball League—"

"National Basketball *Association*!" I said.

"I knew you would catch me on that one," Elijah said. "But dreaming about the National Basketball Association is your business, too, isn't it?"

"I know where this is going, Elijah," I said.

"But our society says that most of the good jobs and nearly all of the best jobs require a college education," Elijah said. "They got it set up so that you can get ahead in certain ways. The tribe did the same thing back in the day. That tribe said that anybody who didn't work didn't eat. Then they said that whoever was the best hunter got his pick of the meat. If you couldn't hunt good, you had to eat the leftovers. That made sense to those cavemen. Make sense to you?"

"You're sounding like a preacher now," I said.

"And if you're strong and you can defend the tribe, then you get to eat with the good hunters," he went on. "That make sense, too?"

"Yeah."

"But today our tribe says that if you're the best hunter, it doesn't mean anything," Elijah said, "because we don't need hunters. And if you're the strongest man on the block, it doesn't mean much, either. Isn't that right?"

"Yeah, that's right," I said.

Elijah had put on a frying pan, put some olive oil in it, and was cooking the cumin seeds. Then he added some garlic, and in a minute the place was smelling good.

"So what we're talking about is society making rules for what it wants done and how it wants to live," Elijah went on. "Some of the things it wants from us are written down like you said, in laws. Laws are the will of the people. But some of the things that aren't written down are also going to dictate how well you do in life."

"Why don't they just write everything down and then everybody would know it and we wouldn't have a problem," I said.

"Because the rules change, sometimes from generation to generation," Elijah said. He was putting the sautéed seeds in a large pot. "Sometimes they change from person to person or from situation to situation. But if you can learn how to tell the differences between onions and maybe make a little soup, you can probably learn a little something about the social contract. What you think?"

"I guess I can," I said.

"The first thing you got to know is that frying up these cumin seeds with a little garlic releases their flavor and adds some depth to our black bean soup we're having this afternoon. Now that's a good thing to know. Did you know that a good black bean soup has more character than some people?"

"I don't mean to be disrespectful, Elijah," I said, "but I don't think I need to know all of this stuff. And what I'm going to say might sound foul, but I don't mean it to be. *Most* people don't go around worrying about ham sandwiches and contracts they don't know about, and they get along just fine."

"Do they, Mr. DuPree?" Elijah asked. "Do they really?"

3

I was supposed to be mentoring some kid on Friday mornings, and I looked forward to it. I figured it would be a boy, maybe a middle school kid having trouble reading. I hoped it wasn't one of those kids who mixed up letters because I didn't think I knew how to deal with that. I arrived at the school at nine thirty and told the guard what I was there for.

"You got ID?" he asked, looking over his glasses at me.

I showed him my ID and he told me to go to the second floor, room 203.

I found the room and there were five kids my age already there and some smaller kids, all boys.

"Mr. DuPree?" A young, thin woman with dark eyes looked up from her clipboard.

"Yes."

"You have to report here every Friday and then go right to the fourth-floor gym," she said. "Keisha's waiting for you there now. You know you're mentoring her in basketball, right?"

"Basketball?"

"She'll explain it," she said. "Have fun."

Basketball? *She'll* explain it? I imagined a nine-year-old on crutches trying to get her confidence up. Okay, I could handle it.

I got to the fourth floor, went to the end of the hall, and saw the school's logo over the entrance to the gym. I walked in and looked around and didn't see any kids. Then I noticed somebody at the water cooler. She was wearing sweats and had a ball under her arm. She saw me and came right over.

"Hey! I'm Keisha. How you doing?"

"I'm doing okay," I said. She looked vaguely familiar, and I knew I had seen her before.

"You know how you got me?" she asked.

"How?" Lame answer, but it was all I could think of.

"I picked you because I saw you play a few times and heard that you were available," she said. "They told you my name? Keisha Marant?"

"Yeah, I mean, no." I was close to stammering. "They said something about basketball."

"Okay, here's the deal," Keisha said. "You want to sit down or something?"

"Yeah, okay."

Now I was remembering who she was. Keisha Marant played ball for George Washington and was All World until she just dropped out of school. Now here she was, all six feet of her, striding over to the benches at the side of the court.

"Here's the deal. They're having a tournament in August down at the Cage on West Fourth Street. I got some girls together who can hoop, and we're going to enter it. I got to show strong and I need some help, so I applied to get myself mentoring when I saw you were in the community program. You don't have that much game, but you can shoot from the outside and that's what I need to work on. You reading me?"

"I thought that mentoring was about reading and math, not basketball," I said.

"So you can't handle it?" Keisha rolled her eyes toward me.

"Yeah, I guess I can handle it," I said. "But I thought your game was already pretty tight?"

"I can play inside, but the college coaches are telling me that they need somebody with an all-around game," Keisha said. "What I'm thinking is that they know I got a baby—"

"You got a baby?"

"They know I got a baby and my grades aren't too tough and I dropped out for a minute, so they think they're taking a chance on recruiting me," she said.

"But if your game is complete, then they'll take that chance," I said, finishing Keisha's thought.

"Then I saw you play and you kept pulling up and popping from the outside," Keisha went on. "I liked the way you looked."

"Okay, let's see how you shoot," I said.

Keisha hunched her shoulders, then dribbled up to the three-point line and let the ball go. The way she shot, I could tell she didn't have any confidence in it going in, and it didn't.

We watched as the ball bounced off the rim, and I retrieved it. I bounced it back to her and nodded toward the basket. She shot again, a two-handed set shot from one side that missed the rim entirely.

"You're too good an athlete to have a shot that bad," I said. "We can make it better if you work at it."

"I'm going to work at it because all I got is basketball," she said. "I ain't got nothing else. I'm not even thinking about going to college unless I have a crutch."

"Basketball?"

"You got it."

"How old are you?"

"Seventeen," Keisha answered. "And don't get any ideas, because I'm not looking for a boyfriend."

Keisha Marant was good-looking. But I didn't know if I could deal with a woman an inch taller than me and maybe a better athlete.

I shot a few times from the top of the key and missed, and she was steady hawking me. The girl was dead serious and I liked that. I did have a good shot, and after a few misses I began dropping them from the three-point line. Every time I looked over at Keisha, she was staring dead at me. It was strange, but it was cool.

"What you need to work on is to shoot with one finger," I said. "You're right-handed, so essentially you shoot with your right index finger. And when you finish the shot, your finger should be pointing at a spot right below the center of the basket. All you really need to do is to get how that feels. And oh, yeah, you need to start the shot higher. If you're strong enough, you can start it from right above your head."

"I'm strong enough!" she said.

"Maybe."

"Maybe? I'm stronger than your little punky butt!" Keisha said. "You want to go one-on-one?"

No, I didn't, but I said yes.

We played to fifteen and she beat me fifteen to seven. Then she said she had to go.

"I thought we were supposed to be dealing for three hours," I said.

"CeCe is with my grandmother, and I have to take care of her," she said.

We started walking toward the door, and I asked her was she coming next week. She said yes, and if things worked out she would stay the whole three hours.

"You know, you can still go to college even if you don't play ball," I said. "I don't think college is that hard."

"It might not be for you, but it will be for me,"

Keisha said. "I don't have a whole lot of discipline and patience and stuff like that. I'm just me doing my thing, and I need some competition or something to keep me going. If I can't play ball, I probably won't be anything any damn way. I know that and you know it, too."

"What do I know about you?" I asked. "I don't know anything about you except you can't shoot from the outside."

"I'm a black seventeen-year-old girl with a baby," Keisha said. "What else do you *need* to know?"

Keisha had an attitude, and she was making sure that I knew it. I didn't know if she could learn to shoot from the outside, but I thought I'd give it my best shot to try to teach her.

I called my friend Terrell and told him what had happened.

"You going to try to get with her?" he asked.

"No, I don't think so," I said.

"Yo, my man is scared!" Terrell's voice went up. "You're scared to try to get with her, man."

"What else do you *need* to know?"

4

It was my second week in Elijah's Soup Emporium, and I was getting used to the routine. Come in at ten, check out what soup Elijah was cooking, start getting ready for the next day's soup. When the seniors came in at noon, me and Elijah would serve them, then take their plates when they had finished. Elijah would work on the next day's soup in the afternoon while I did the washing. I was liking Elijah, too. He was always kidding me, but I felt that he had accepted me right away. I realized he was trying to teach me things—no, more than that. He was trying to pass on things he knew.

"That's sixteen regulars and four new people," Elijah said when the last of the seniors had left for the day. "Not bad for summer. When the weather gets cold, we're going to have close to forty or fifty people coming in for a bowl of soup."

"It was good soup, too," I said.

"I know it was," Elijah answered. "If there's anything in this world that I do know, it's the difference between good soup and dishwater."

"What kind of soup we making this afternoon?" I asked.

"I don't make too many different kinds of soup here," Elijah said, cutting up some more onions, which, I think, was his favorite thing to do. "We serve five days a week, and so we have five basic soups and three once-in-a-while soups. Tomorrow the soup is collard greens and ham in beef stock. In the winter, we serve the same soup with a few white beans added for weight."

"Collard greens *soup*?" I asked. "I never heard of it."

"Hasn't it come to you yet, Mr. DuPree, that there are more than one or two things you haven't heard of in this life?" Elijah asked me.

I was trying to think of something good to say when the doorbell rang. Miss Watkins was a regular at the soup kitchen. She always brought her own cloth napkin, which she would spread on her lap before being served. She looked me up and down and then waved a thin dark hand for me to move aside. I stepped back, and she came in and spoke to Elijah.

"I'm going down to the fish market on 125th Street," she said. "You needing anything?"

"See if they got some fresh mullet," Elijah said. "I can use a few pounds. What are you doing out here in all this heat, Miss Watkins?"

"Walking off the rust spots," Miss Watkins said. "Can't let myself get too stiff to be about my business."

Elijah gave Miss Watkins five dollars for the mullets and asked if she needed anything.

"Just need enough to do to keep the grave from tempting me," Miss Watkins said.

She took one of Elijah's cloth shopping bags with her, to carry the fish in, and left.

"That woman has seen more in her lifetime than anybody needs to be seeing," Elijah said. "Good-hearted woman, too. She lost her husband in the war, and a daughter two years later in a house fire. You don't see many people who have been through as much as she's experienced who haven't grown hard-hearted."

"You think she knows about your social contract?" I asked.

"Maybe, maybe not," Elijah said. "She might not have the vocabulary in place, but she's living out her relationship with the world just as nice as you please."

"Okay, so you're the man as far as soup goes," I said. "But I was thinking about those cavemen you were talking about the other day. If that contract thing you talking about was so tough, then how come the cavemen aren't around anymore?"

"What makes you think the cavemen aren't around anymore?" Elijah asked. "Just because they dress different than what you see in the movies?"

"You mean they dress different but they're still around with the same contract?" I asked.

"No, they turned in that old contract for a new one," Elijah said. "Now put these greens in the sink and wash them good."

"They look clean to me," I said. "I think they wash them in the vegetable market."

"Mr. DuPree, please do an old man a favor," Elijah said, speaking slowly. "I know you're sitting on that stool to keep it from floating away, but get up and go wash the greens as I asked you."

Washing collard greens isn't too bad because the leaves are broad and you just have to run water over them to wash away any grit that might be left on them. I started doing that while Elijah cut up the ham shoulder.

"Did you invent collard greens soup?" I asked.

"No, but I was raised on it," Elijah said. "Way back in slavery days, the only things that people had to eat was what they could raise themselves and what the master gave them. Collard greens were a good, healthy crop. If they could get a piece of smoked pork to season it, then they were doing all right. The right stuff for eating didn't have to be expensive."

"The right stuff?"

"That's what we're doing, Mr. DuPree," Elijah said. "We're taking all the right stuff, putting it together, and making something wonderful."

"You mean the soups?" I asked. "Or you mean bringing people together?"

"Boy, did you just grow a few inches right in front of my eyes?"

"What you mean?"

"What I mean is that you're a pretty sharp young man," Elijah said. "I'm going to have to get a little deeper with my social contract theories with you."

"Yeah, okay," I said. "But check this out. I had American history in the seventh and ninth grades. We didn't have anything about social contracts. And we didn't have anything about cavemen in America, either."

"All right, I'll take back what I said about you growing," Elijah said. "But some men in England way back in the thirteenth century started talking about a social contract—"

"No, I said America," I said. "You know, the United States."

"Kings and queens and lords and ladies and barons and whatnot," Elijah said, ignoring me. "And these men looked around and noticed that the king had all the rights and the barons wanted some for themselves. If the king said jump, you said, 'How high?' If the king said, 'Lay down and die,' you laid down and at least closed your eyes. So some fellows got together and talked about getting a set of rules to give all free men an even break. What they dreamed of was a contract that restricted some of the powers of the king.

"And the king was all right with that?"

"Well, he was all right with it when he saw that the people were thinking about cutting his head off if he wasn't all right with it," Elijah said, grinning.

"That was over in England someplace?"

"Yes, it was. But after that, the English started thinking that they could influence the way government worked and began trying to make laws based on what they thought was fair for everybody," Elijah said.

"That was good," I said.

"To a point," Elijah said. "It was good in some ways and bad in other ways."

"How come nothing I say is completely right?" I asked Elijah.

He turned slowly and looked at me. "I was wondering about that myself," he said.

Just then a knock came on the door, and a shiny-faced brother asked if Tony was in.

"Tony lives on the next floor," Elijah said. "You can go up there and play as many numbers as you want and leave as much money with Tony as you need to."

The shiny-faced brother looked at me, then looked at Elijah, touched the front of his cap, and walked away.

"Tony's the local numbers man," Elijah said. "Part of the shady side of Harlem. Meanwhile, are you giving them greens a bubble bath or are you just washing them?"

I took the greens out of the water and took the knife that Elijah handed me and started chopping them. He took the knife from me and chopped some to show me how he wanted it done and then handed it back to me again. I started chopping, and he grunted, which I figured meant I was doing it right.

"Things were better over in England after they restricted the king's powers. Laws were made to enforce the social contract, but there were still some people down at the bottom of the ladder, struggling in the mud, trying to get out of the mess they were in. Some other people just didn't like how the country was being run, and so they decided to leave and come over to where a new land had been discovered. That land they were calling America."

"The Pilgrims," I said.

"Some of them were Pilgrims," Elijah said. "Some were just people looking to start their lives over again. Some were convicts sent over here in place of being sent to jail or hanged. They started landing over here around 1600. Soon as they got over here, they started making their own social contract. They figured what was going to be the best thing for their society, and they created rules and laws that had to be followed."

"Which was the right thing to do," I said.

"In a way it was, and in a way it wasn't," Elijah said.

"That's because you can't let me get one point in that's right," I said.

"No, Mr. DuPree," Elijah said. "Because life is never that simple. You see, when all those folks arrived here from England, there were already some people living here. You might have heard of them. The Erie, the Seminole, the Mohawk, and out west, the Navajo, the Hopi, the Comanche, and so forth."

"The Indians?"

"The so-called Indians," Elijah said. "Now the people living here had their own social contracts that suited them just fine. But the people coming from England decided that their social contract was the best one and the people already living here had to move aside. The people from England had the most guns, and their social contracts started to win out."

"Whoa, wait a minute." I stopped chopping greens. "When you were running down the social contract the other day—that was the ham sandwich business—you were talking about people agreeing to stuff. Now you're talking about this king over in England, and he was being forced to deal with the contract. Then you get over to America, and you're talking about who's got the most guns. That's not a contract, brother, that's intimidation."

"That's true, Mr. DuPree, that's definitely true."

"Yo, Elijah, you leading me through a whole lot of mess that you're saying is about the social contract, but I'm thinking it's about people doing what they want to do."

"But is it history?" Elijah asked. "Did it really happen?"

"Yeah."

"Then it's worth looking at, isn't it?"

"You know, I don't know if I should feel glad that you're running this down to me," I said, "or mad because of the way it went down!"

"That's why we need people with intelligence and a good sense of justice to pay close attention to the social contract and the theories behind it," Elijah said. "An Englishman named John Locke said that property was not just land but the labor used to develop that land as well. So if the Indians weren't cultivating that land, it was all right for the Europeans on the scene to take it."

"Get out of here!"

"You think I'm not telling you the truth?"

"So the people from England just decided that their contract was going to be the bomb and they forced it on everybody else?"

"There were really a number of social contracts going on at the same time," Elijah said. "And that's always the case, Paul. There was the one contract for the well-off white men; there was one for white women; there was one for Native Americans and another for people from Africa. But the one with the most weight was the one for white men, because that gave them all the advantages they thought were their due, and that was the best way for their society to get on with their business."

"Yo, Elijah, I think you just messed up my whole day!"

"Now you're learning, boy. Put those greens in that big pot and then reach under the cupboard there and get a fourteen-ounce can of tomatoes and add that to the pot," Elijah said. "That's to get some acid on the greens. Some people put vinegar in their greens, but you don't want vinegar in your soup, do you?"

I opened the can and put the tomatoes in one of Elijah's huge pots. He had finished cutting up the ham he wanted—it looked like about a half pound—and he added that to the tomatoes.

"You want me to stir it?" I asked.

"No, Mr. DuPree, I think you're stirred up enough for one day. It'll let you know when it's ready for stirring," Elijah said.

"Okay now, where were we? Oh, yes, it's around 1775, and the British men are getting restless. They're thinking that they're under Great Britain's thumb, and they're tired of it."

"1775?"

"That's right, and you know what happened next?"

"The Revolutionary War," I said.

"All those people standing up in Philadelphia and Boston and New York talking about how they needed to be free," Elijah said. "It makes your head spin and your heart light just to read their speeches or hear somebody recite them. They were forging themselves a new social contract. A lot of the stuff in the new contract was the same as the old deal, but a few things were different. They were going to make sure that everybody would have some kind of voice in the government. What's more, the people of this country were going to elect their ruler. What's that called?"

"A democracy," I said.

"No, sir, that's called a lie," Elijah said. "Women couldn't vote, children couldn't vote, and black people couldn't vote. So what they were really saying was that the white men in this country were going to rule it."

"So the social contract is about getting over on everybody else," I said. "I know you're going to say that's wrong, because that's your nature, but that's the way I see it."

"That's the way a lot of people see it," Elijah said. "They think that there can't really be a social contract because somewhere along the way, somebody is being forced to accept it. But people over the years who have been thinking about this idea of a social contract think we can do a lot better than just 'getting over.' They break it down to the two points we've been discussing all along. And when you think about them, they make a lot of good sense. If you learn these two points, then you got something going for yourself."

"So what are they?" I asked.

"The first point is that you can do anything your mind can dream up and your body can perform," Elijah said. "Just anything in the world."

"We're getting back to the ham sandwich?"

"That we are," Elijah said, nodding slightly. "And the second point is that you give up that right to do anything you want because you've figured out that there's a better way for society to function."

"I can go for it. But you just ran down to me that the people who came to America back in the day messed over the people already living here," I said. "And I know all about slavery, and I know no brothers from Africa signed a contract saying they didn't want to be free."

"It must be the aroma from the collard greens," Elijah said, "because your thinking is getting clearer and clearer."

"Yo, and let me run down something else," I said. "Say you have a thousand dudes living on an island, right?"

"Go on," Elijah said.

"And they're happy with their little social contract, and all of them are getting the same amount of food to eat, and the same television channels, and the same amount of minutes on their cell phones, okay?"

"Go on, Mr. DuPree."

"I think there would still be a problem," I said. "Because sooner or later one of those people would figure out that he could live a little better than the others if he could find a way to take somebody else's food or snatch up their cell phone minutes. That's the way people are!"

"That's true, Mr. DuPree," Elijah said. "So we need to watch each other very closely. When we elect a government, we need to watch that government very closely and know exactly how it's supposed to be working. You don't enter a contract with your eyes closed."

"I don't know if this social contract business is good or bad," I said.

"You'll make up your mind sooner or later," Elijah said. "Sooner or later."

I knew I would if he had anything to do with it.

We served the soup, and I listened as Miss Watkins told about how her husband had been wounded in the Second World War and Mr. Pickens said he had been drafted to go to Korea but got out of it because he had a bad eye.

"You should have served your country," Miss Watkins said. "And you should have been proud to do it!"

Miss Watkins was a feisty old lady and I liked her. In fact, I liked most of the seniors who came to Elijah's. What I thought was that they liked Elijah and felt good being there. I was feeling good about being there myself.

5

I met up with Terrell and we walked down to Morningside Park to play some ball. We got into a few games and got creamed. Terrell's game was never that good, but somehow he was getting worse. He was almost as tall as me, and I thought he was getting out of shape.

"We should have won that last game," Terrell said as we turned up my block.

"We would have won if you passed the ball once in a while," I said. "You were shooting with two and three guys hanging on your arm."

"Yo, man, I was in the zone!"

"In the zone?" I watched as Terrell went up for an imaginary jump shot. "You weren't even in the right zip code!"

"Yeah, yeah," Terrell said. "I had to hurry my shots because you weren't getting any rebounds."

"I don't even see how that works together," I said, wondering how my rebounding made him hurry his shots.

"Hey, check this out!" Terrell lowered his voice. "Ain't that D-Boy across the street?"

I looked across the street and saw D-Boy sitting on a stoop. He had his do-rag down across his forehead, almost to his shades. I looked at my side of the street and saw Sly standing on my stoop.

Everybody knew Sly and nobody knew Sly. He was around the hood a lot and rode in a fantastic machine, and D-Boy was his bodyguard. Some people thought he was into drugs and some said he was part of the black mafia. Everybody gave the dude his propers and nobody moved up on him too quick. He had known my father and had sent flowers to the funeral.

"Don't say nothing stupid," I said to Terrell.

"I'm not," Terrell said, voice low, eyes getting big. "I heard that D-Boy will shoot you if you even look hard at Sly."

We had reached my stoop, and I asked Terrell if he wanted to come in.

"No, I got to pick up my sister from church," he answered.

"She goes to church in the evenings?" I asked.

"The building fund has a meeting," he said. "I'll call you later."

Terrell lived on the hill. I watched him walk to the corner, and then I started walking into my building.

"Hey, Paul, what you doing with your young self?" Sly was about six feet two, well built, and wore frameless glasses on the end of his nose.

"Same old, same old," I said.

"You need to make twenty-five dollars in a hurry?" Sly asked. He had a toothpick in the corner of his mouth.

"No."

"Why, you got rich since the last time I saw you?" Sly looked at me sideways.

"I got a job," I said. "It gets me over."

"Where you working?"

"At a soup kitchen," I said. "Well, sort of a soup kitchen. This guy makes soup every day for senior citizens."

"You talking about Elijah Jones's place on 144th Street, across from the school?" Sly asked.

"Yeah, you know him?"

"Yeah, I know him," Sly said. "Old man, got that old man thing going on. You know, catch some holiness before he passes on. What do they say these days? Getting right before the sunset."

"He's okay," I said.

"He's talking to you about Jesus and getting saved?" Sly asked.

"No, about something called the social contract," I said.

"The social contract?" Sly's eyes kept shifting up and down the street. "Yeah, yeah, I'm hip to that scene."

"No, this isn't like a real contract—" I started.

"It's an agreement between people to surrender some of their rights so that they can live in peace with one another," Sly said. "That's what he told you?"

"You know about the social contract?"

"I don't go around in a cap and gown, so I'm supposed to be stupid or something?" Sly asked.

"I didn't say that," I said.

"I studied the social contract at Grambling," Sly said. "But when I see young brothers like you scared to make twenty-five dollars, I can tell it's not working.

The social contract has you running scared, right?"

"No." I could feel my heart beating faster.

"Yeah, it does," Sly said. "That's what it's supposed to do. Set up a bunch of rules so that some people can stay on top and be comfortable while people like you and me can learn to get comfortable on the bottom. Elijah's making the bottom feel good, but it's still the bottom."

"I see you've been talking to him," I said.

"I used to rap to him some when I was your age," Sly said. "Liked him, too. He taught history in the public school system and did odd jobs to make enough money to buy a little real estate. I saw how he and a whole lot of people like him went around smiling and telling people how they're blessed."

"I don't think he's that religious," I said.

"Yeah, he is." Sly checked his watch. "You scratch a do-gooder and they got a religious streak somewhere in them. So you want to make the twenty-five dollars or not?"

"What do I have to do?"

"First, wipe the scared look off your face," Sly said, smiling. "The cops see a black teenager walking down the street looking scared, they're liable to arrest you on the spot. Then go to the corner store, buy a bottle of soda, and go up to Broadhurst Avenue and give it to the first brother you see looks like he can use a cold drink. Then come back here and tell me what he said when you gave him the soda."

"That's all?"

"That's all," Sly said.

Sly went into his pocket and pulled out a five-dollar bill and handed it to me. I was scared to take it and scared not to take it. I wanted to look over at D-Boy to see what he was doing, but I didn't want Sly to see me doing it.

Finally I took the money, then I took a deep breath and walked to the corner store. I could feel Sly's eyes following me, and I couldn't even walk cool. I bought the soda, made sure it was cold, then took it up the hill.

Broadhurst was crowded, but I saw a dude who looked kind of down and out, and I walked up to him.

"Yo, you want a soda?"

He took the soda and just looked at me.

"So, what you got to say?" I asked him as he twisted the cap off the soda.

He took a long, slow drink, then gave me a mean look. "I ain't saying nothing," he said. "I didn't ask you for no soda."

"Okay." I shrugged and turned.

"Yo, pretty boy!"

I turned back.

"Go to hell!" he said.

I went on back down the hill and saw that Sly was still on the stoop. All the way down the hill, I was looking for plainclothes cops. I was thinking that me taking that soda up the hill might have been a signal that the coast was clear or something or some big drug deal was going to go down.

When I got to the stoop, I handed Sly back his change.

"What did he say?" Sly asked.

"First he said he didn't ask me for a soda so he didn't have to say nothing," I said. "Then he thought about it and said, 'Go to hell!'"

"What he was saying was that if you got money, you can look down on folks and act like you're doing them a favor," Sly said. "But that brother knew that when you left, he still was going to be standing there and still didn't have anything going on. And he wasn't buying into your social contract, either. He just wanted to let you know that. Here's your twenty-five dollars."

"That's okay," I said.

"No, it's not okay," Sly said. He put the money into my shirt pocket. "When a young man is afraid to deal with his fellow man, it means the system has you so brainwashed that you're afraid to follow your mind. You put your mind in your pocket and follow the system. The same system that your friend Elijah is calling the social contract.

"You think you know something when you're talking about philosophy, but that brother you gave the soda to knows a lot more than you."

Sly stepped off the stoop and got into a car I hadn't seen pull up. He rolled the window down and beckoned for me to come over to the car.

"So you know all about the social contract, Rousseau, Hobbes, and all those old dudes?" he asked.

"I know some about it," I said. "I don't know those guys you're talking about. But I think I would like to know more."

"That's good," Sly said. "Only fools don't want to learn more about everything."

He rolled up the window. And he was gone.

I really had to pee bad.

I wondered what Sly thought about my father. He thought the dude who told me to go to hell knew something. Maybe he would have thought my father knew something, too.

6

I knew that Elijah was laying traps for me. Old people like to do that to young people. They set you up to say something and then jump all over it. I thought what Elijah said was interesting, and the way he said it, talking about ham sandwiches and stuff, was funny. But thinking about it when he wasn't around was still confusing. When I got to the emporium in the morning, I had a bunch of questions ready for Elijah.

"The way I figure it," I said after I walked through the door, "is that either everybody follows the social contract bit or nobody follows it. I'm not going to play by some rules if there are people going around doing what they want to do."

"Good morning, Mr. DuPree," Elijah said. "I see

that young mind of yours has been working overtime. It's got you so riled up, you can skip right past 'good morning.'"

"Good morning, sir," I said. "But I mean what I said. About the ham sandwich. I think if somebody takes my sandwich, I should feel free to take theirs."

"The soup of the day is oxtail," Elijah said. "It's been on since five this morning and it's smelling pretty good. Did you know there was a time you could buy oxtails for twenty cents a pound? They were the same as bones or spare ribs. Now they cost you as much as prime beef."

"Well, I guess maybe there's a shortage of oxen," I said. "The less there is of something, the more it costs."

"Oxtails don't have anything to do with oxen," Elijah said. "They have to do with cows and bulls. It just doesn't sound so good saying 'bull tail,' now does it?"

"No, sir, it doesn't."

"Now getting back to what you were saying about the social contract." Elijah slowly stirred the soup and waved his hand over the large pot to get some of the smell. He looked at me and smiled, and I knew he thought he had made some good soup. "I agree with you one hundred percent. If anybody walks away from the social contract, then we should all walk away. I think that Thursdays and Fridays are the best days. What do you think?"

"The best days for what?"

"For robbing and killing people and taking their ham sandwiches or their money or their televisions," Elijah said. "Because that's what we're talking about, aren't we? Killing people and taking their stuff?"

"I didn't say that, Elijah, and you know it," I said. "What I mean is that if somebody is going to think it's okay to take my stuff, then, you know . . ."

"What do I know?" Elijah asked. "I know a lot of people believe they should be able to follow wherever the wind pushes them. Look at all the fellows and gals in prisons and jails today. Ninety-nine point nine percent of them are stone guilty, and they know it. They have wiped their feet on the social contract. You look at them close, and all their lips are greasy from somebody else's ham sandwich. And now you're telling me that because they're doing it, then you got to do it, too."

"You hear me say that?" I asked. "Because I didn't hear me say that. What I said was if you're going to take my stuff, then I think that I have the right to take yours."

"I'm agreeing with you. I'm on your side. Now let's me and you look around and see who is not doing their part on the social contract we're talking about," Elijah said. "We got all these people running around stealing and shooting people. How about them?"

"They're not following the social contract," I said.

"How about the people doing the kidnapping and the hijacking?" Elijah asked. "What we going to do about them?"

"They're not following the contract," I said.

"How about the woman who fakes a fall in the department store so she can sue and get some money?" Elijah asked.

"What you mean, how about her?" I asked.

"Well, she's stealing from the insurance company, which is going to raise your rates, so that's a good thing or a bad thing?" Elijah asked.

"That's a bad thing," I said.

"That enough for you to throw away your copy of the contract?"

"Not by itself, but if everybody is doing it . . . that's different," I said. "The Bible says, 'Do unto others as you would have others do unto you.'"

"I'm glad you're reading the Good Book, Mr. DuPree," Elijah said. "But that doesn't stop me from not knowing whether you're going to follow the social contract or not. Because it seems to me like you're looking around to see what everybody else is doing first, and then making up your mind as things go along."

"You have to do that," I said. "Don't you have a right to protect yourself?"

"A fundamental, inalienable right, sir," Elijah said. "You certainly have a right to protect yourself and what belongs to you. But what you're telling me is that if everybody in the tribe doesn't follow the contract, then there can't be a contract, and that bothers me. It bothers me because there's always somebody who wants to walk their own way, or who looks at the contract and says, 'Hey, I can get an advantage out of this situation.'"

"Okay, so I know this guy who was telling me that all the social contract does is to make little people like me scared to step out of line so the people in charge can do whatever they want to do," I said. "And he studied the social contract in college."

"So he should know something about it," Elijah said.

"He does know something about it," I said. "I was thinking about what he said and what you said and it's almost the same thing, but he looks at it differently than you do. You said we were giving up our right to do anything we wanted, and Sly said the same thing, except he was saying that the people on top never have to give up their rights, just the people on the bottom."

"Hobbes," Elijah said. "A lot of people study Hobbes, but they don't really understand him."

"I'm talking about Sly," I said. "He's a big dude, wears those little glasses."

"I'm talking about Thomas Hobbes," Elijah said. "He was one of the first men to talk about the social contract. You can look him up on the internet."

"You use the internet?"

"Mr. DuPree, I am a black man with gray hair, a touch of arthritis, and a thirst for knowledge. I am not a dinosaur!"

"Yes, sir."

"And this fellow you're talking about is right. Hobbes was trying to make sense of how people can live together successfully, but he thought that most people couldn't make their own decisions. In his version of the social contract, the people on top of the heap had to decide the best way for society to live. If you let people make their own decisions, life would end up being poor, nasty, and short."

"That's what Sly said!"

"When you say Sly, are you referring to Mr. Edward Norton? Young man who drives around in a fancy car and has a bodyguard?" Elijah asked.

"He said he used to talk to you," I answered. "You know him?"

"I know his family and yes, I used to talk to him at times," Elijah said. "His father was a preacher, and so was his grandfather. Edward, or Sly, as he likes to be called, was always a bright young man. But one morning he got up and looked in the mirror and saw himself in a new light. He saw the same thing that a lot of other people, including Hobbes, saw—that maybe the social contract was good for most people, but the people on top didn't really have to worry about the people on the bottom."

"And Sly sees himself as one of the people on the top?"

"That he does, Mr. DuPree. That he does. But

Edward is a young man who thinks, and that's good."

"So does this all end up with somebody being right and somebody being wrong?" I asked.

"It ends up with people looking at the same picture and seeing different things," Elijah said. "A man named John Rawls said that the only way that the social contract could work perfectly was if everybody goes into it blind. And our friend Edward—or Sly, as you call him—is not going to close his eyes for a minute."

"I like my problems easier," I said. "I don't mind thinking about things, but I want to come up with an answer."

"Let's have a fancy tablecloth today," Elijah said. "You go upstairs and go into the room on the right-hand side of the hallway. Inside you'll find a breakfront, glass doors on top and drawers on the bottom. Look in the top drawer, and you'll see two real nice light-blue tablecloths. Bring them down and we'll set the tables.

"And take your time going up and down the stairs," Elijah went on. "Because I need you to figure out for me if right needs to be right for everybody and for all time, and if wrong for you is always wrong for me."

"Yo, Elijah, no offense, sir, but I'm not going there," I said. "My head is already spinning around this social contract stuff. If I try to get any deeper in this mess, I'm liable to rupture my brain or something."

After I got the tablecloths, I washed and dried the tables. Then me and Elijah laid out the cloths and smoothed them over. Elijah's got a lot of different sets of plates, and this time he used the ones with the blue border and gold trim. When the people started coming in, they all noticed how nice the tables looked, and Mr. Perkins said it reminded him of his aunt Mae's table down in Camden, New Jersey.

"Elijah, you put wine in this soup?" Sister Effie was about nine hundred years old. "Because I don't drink wine and I don't want no wine in my soup!"

"No wine, Effie," Elijah said. "Just oxtails, carrots, and good stock."

Everybody left happy. Miss Lou Fennell, who was kind of sick and who couldn't speak, came over and patted Elijah's hand and then patted mine.

I washed the dishes, put the tablecloths in the washing machine, and cleaned the kitchen as Elijah looked over the vegetables he was going to use in tomorrow's soup.

Before I left, I got the spelling of Hobbes from Elijah. At home, I looked him up and got a zillion hits! I looked at a few of them and saw that people were not only writing about Thomas Hobbes but discussing the social contract all over the internet. What came to me was that if that many people were all over the social contract, how come almost nobody who I knew was down with it?

"There's a girl on the phone," Mom said. "She sounds young."

It was Keisha. She asked what I was doing.

"Nothing much," I said.

"I got to take CeCe to the hospital," she said. "You know how long they take in the emergency room. Why don't you come over and sit with me?"

"What hospital?"

"Harlem, on 135th Street."

"Yeah, okay."

"Fifteen minutes," she said, and then hung up before I had a chance to answer.

"Who was it?" Mom asked.

"Remember that girl I told you I was mentoring on Fridays?"

"That's not *mentoring*!" Mom said. "Basketball isn't mentoring."

"She thinks it'll get her into college," I said, putting on my jacket.

"Where you going?"

"To the hospital," I said. "Her baby is sick and she wants me to sit with her in the waiting room."

"Her *baby*?" Mom's eyebrows arched. "She goes to high school and she's got a baby. You're teaching her basketball and now you're helping her take care of the baby. How well do you know her, Paul?"

"Hey, it's no big thing," I said. "A lot of girls have babies before they finish high school."

"It should be a big thing," Mom said. "You watch yourself."

"Yes, ma'am."

When I got over to Harlem Hospital, I saw Keisha waiting in the lobby. She had her little girl on her hip.

"She's cute," I said. "What's wrong with her?"

"Asthma," Keisha said. "Soon as she starts breathing funny, I take her to the hospital. My girlfriend's baby had an attack once and she didn't take her to the hospital. She waited until the next morning, and the baby died."

"From *asthma*? You can die from asthma?"

"Yes, you can die from asthma."

We went to the emergency room, and Keisha told the receptionist what was wrong. Then she sat down with me.

CeCe was big, with a perfectly round face and wide eyes that made her look like a doll. She wasn't coughing but making a whistling noise with her breath, and she seemed to be having a hard time.

"How old is she?" I asked.

"Almost two," Keisha said. "She developed asthma about six months ago. The doctor said she might outgrow it. A lot of kids do."

The waiting room was full. One guy was in his undershirt, and a woman next to him had her arm around him. Another dude's face was all swollen on one side, and he had a cut over his eye. He looked as if he had been beaten up.

There were so many people in the waiting area that some people had to stand. What you did was wait until your name appeared on a board, and then you went into another room. I didn't know what they did in there.

A Latino guy was doubled over across from where

me and Keisha sat, moaning and holding his stomach. Next to him was a skinny girl—she could have been a crackhead—with her head back and her mouth open. A teenage guy was with an older woman, and she was complaining about how long they had been waiting.

"If we were in a white neighborhood, they would see us right away," she said. "His arm is probably broken and they just don't care."

"How you hurt your arm?" Keisha asked the teenager.

"Playing touch football," the boy said, smiling. "I caught the ball, though."

The moaning guy stood up and started toward the door, but stopped and threw up before he made it out of the room.

"Damn!" An old man I hadn't noticed before called out. "Now we got to sit here and smell his puke!"

The guy who had thrown up gave the old man a dirty look and the finger and left the room. The receptionist made a phone call, and soon a janitor came in and cleaned up the mess.

"Can anybody come and see about my grandson?" the woman asked the receptionist.

"No, the doctors are all in the back playing

poker," the receptionist said.

"I believe you, too!" the old woman said.

Just then the door opened and a small crowd of people came in. The Latino man who had thrown up came in first and sat back down where he had been before. Then a pale woman came in, supported by a man who could have been her husband, and two cops, with a man in handcuffs.

"Gunshot wound!" the younger cop announced.

The receptionist got up, opened the frosted door to the next room, and the cops went through with the handcuffed man.

"Now we got to wait for the perp to get taken care of," the old man said from the corner. "If the damned cops could shoot straight, they would have killed him and we wouldn't be delayed."

Some of the people laughed at that, even the sick Latino.

CeCe started breathing hard, and Keisha patted her on her back and held her close.

I bet none of these people knew anything about Elijah's social contract. Maybe Sly was right, that it really wasn't meant for people like the ones in the emergency room. These people were sick, maybe even dying, and they had to wait to get seen and sit in the small room as if they somehow belonged together. And the old man was right—the smell of the puke and the disinfectant or whatever they had put on it was stinking up the joint.

"What are you thinking about so deep?" Keisha asked.

"About making soup and the social contract," I said.

"You're a little girlish, aren't you?"

"Nah, I don't think so," I said. "In the Soup Emporium—in the soup kitchen—I work in, the old man talks a lot about the social contract. Do you know what the social contract is?"

"No, and I don't want to know, either," Keisha said.

I looked at her to see if she was kidding. She wasn't. "Why?" I asked. "You want to go to college and make something of yourself, so why don't you want to know what the social contract is?"

"Paul, and I don't particularly like your name, either," Keisha said, "my life is simple. I either make it to the WNBA and make a bunch of money to take care of myself and CeCe, or I spend the rest of my life kissing tail and hoping for the best. I've watched you play ball. Your first step sucks because you don't *need* a first step. You got smarts backing you up, and probably a good family."

"My father was killed this year," I said. "When he was alive, he wasn't with us."

"What did he have going on?"

"Not much," I said. "In and out of the slam, mostly. Maybe he was trying to get himself together at the end, I don't know."

"That's what's wrong in the hood," Keisha said. "We're looking around for our fathers instead of looking up to them. I think you're okay, though. I'd like to marry somebody like you someday. But I really don't think it's going to happen. I don't."

She turned away, and we sat there for an hour more waiting for her name to be called. Finally she went in, carrying CeCe on her hip. She said I didn't have to wait if I didn't want to.

Keisha's attitude was weird, but it was sounding enough like what Sly was saying to have some weight to it. He had been talking about people at the bottom of society having to stay there. And looking around the waiting room, I saw people who didn't look like they were ever going to be anyplace but where they were right then, lining up looking for some help.

I stood up and let some of the new people sit down. The guy the cops had brought had his side covered with a big bandage.

"They shot me and I didn't do nothing!" he called out to anyone who wanted to listen.

"Should have shot you in the head!" the old man in the corner shouted back. "Save the taxpayers some money!"

I waited for Keisha and CeCe and thought about what she had said about me not needing a first step. I wondered if she believed that, or was she just being Keisha-tough? She *had* called me to go to the hospital with her. It was strange how beat down the people in the waiting room looked—not just sick, or hurt, but beat down.

When she came out, she had a bag with two emergency inhalers for the baby.

"She going to be all right?"

"Yeah," Keisha said. "Thanks for waiting."

Keisha lived on 160th Street. She had the money for a cab and dropped me off on 145th. I felt bad for her and for CeCe, but when the little girl smiled at me, I felt better.

7

"So let's say that you and your friend Sly live right next door to each other," Elijah said. "And you have three million dollars in the bank, and he has three million dollars. You have a big house, and he's got a big house. You have a fancy car, and he's got a fancy car. And then one day, you leave your house to go downtown and forget about a bottle of soda on your patio table. Do you think that Sly is going to come over and steal your soda?"

"In the first place, he's not my friend," I said. "I just see him around the hood. But if he's got three million dollars, I don't think he's going to come to my house and snatch a soda."

"So what you're saying is that when everybody is rich and safe and has as much as they need, they don't think much about the social contract," Elijah said. He was preparing carrots and lentils for his harira soup. "Most Americans don't think about the social contract, but we're all still dealing with it. We have a police force that's going to protect everybody, and an army, and rules and regulations. So even if they're not signing a formal agreement called the social contract, it's still there for them."

"How did you get all up into thinking like this?" I asked.

"My grandfather lived in Littig, a small colored town in Texas. When he was growing up there, just about everybody in the town was black, and some of the older folks had been slaves. He said they had a few white people in town, and the whites and the coloreds got along just fine. In Littig, they had three kinds of food. They had pinch food, which you ate just to keep your stomach from pinching. That was mostly potatoes or rice, pan bread, greens, and whatever you could hunt up. He said you would go to somebody's house and find a mess of squirrel stew on the stove, or coon, or wild birds. If you could hunt, you could eat.

"Then there was step-up food. You were happy with

your step-up food because you knew you were eating good. Beef was plentiful, but he didn't get much in the way of steaks and what have you. Mostly he had oxtails, shanks, and a little stew once in a while."

"Hamburgers," I said. "They're made of beef."

"That's true," Elijah said. "But you know I never had a hamburger until I came up north? Didn't know what the things were, and I know my grandfather didn't."

"What was the other kind of food?" I asked.

"High life," Elijah said, smiling. "That meant you were eating parts of animals that weren't that close to the ground. Instead of trotters, which is the pig's feet, you were eating pork shoulder and chops. Instead of eating chicken-feet soup—"

"Chicken-feet soup?"

"Boy, I've eaten more chicken feet in my life than I've eaten anything else," Elijah said. "Boil 'em up for a few hours with some dumplings, cut up a potato or two in the pot, add a couple of tablespoons of flour and some salt and pepper, and you got the makings for a cold winter night."

"I'm going to pass on the chicken feet," I said.

"Well, I'm sure the chickens will appreciate that,

Mr. DuPree," Elijah said. "But as I moved on through life, I began to notice that some folks stayed on the chicken-feet level all their lives. Some moved up to chopsville, and some just seemed to do well all the time. They ate first-rate food, lived well, and didn't seem to have the troubles the chicken-feet people had. And I began wondering if there was a cause to that."

"That's what Sly was saying," I said. "Why are some people always on the bottom?"

"I wondered, same as he did, if there was something going on that I didn't know about. And what I figured out, sir, was that people find themselves part of a social order and don't understand what that order is or what they need to do to make it work for them," Elijah said. "There are rules—sometimes they are laws and sometimes they are just the way things are done—that affect how we all live."

"Sly was right on that," I said.

"No, he thinks there's a plot out there to keep certain people down," Elijah said. "What I'm saying is that there's a plot to help everybody in a certain way. And if you're not smart enough to figure out that way, then you are no better off than the crabs I told you about. I did tell you about the crabs, didn't I?"

"No, but I'm sure you will."

"Once upon a time, there were three little crabs swimming off the eastern shore of Maryland. The three crabs were named Billy Joe, Billy Bob, and Billy Come-Along. All day long these three little crabs would swim in the water right behind their mother. The first crab, Billy Joe, held on to his mother with one claw. The second crab, Billy Bob, would be holding on to Billy Joe, and Billy Come-Along would be holding on to him. When the mother crab would find some sea grub or something like that, she would eat part of it and give the rest to her little babies.

"One day they were swimming near the pier when the mother crab saw a small trout caught in a trap. Well, she hadn't had any trout for a long time.

"She went over to where the trout was lying in the trap. *Kerblam!*" Elijah clapped his hands together. "That trap closed, and pretty soon it was being pulled out of the water. The three little crabs didn't much know what to do, and in truth, there wasn't much they could do. Their mama was gone. How were they going to get along all by themselves?"

"The first crab, Billy Joe, looked up and saw a bird

flying in the air. He said that looked like something he would like to do, and he climbed out of the water, went up the biggest mountain he could find, and jumped. Killed him stone dead.

"The second crab, Billy Bob, saw a man walking his dog along the riverbank. Billy Bob thought that looked like a good thing to do, so he got out and walked along the riverbank, too. When the dog saw Billy Bob, he ran over and bit him in the back. Killed him stone dead.

"Now Billy Come-Along had seen all this and was a little nervous. At first he decided to stay right there in the water. But by this time, he was hungry. He swam over to the pier, and he saw a trout tied to another trap. He went over to get himself some trout while he thought things over, and *kerblam!* He was caught in that trap.

"The man who had laid out the crab traps had his idea of what a good social contract was. The crabs had their idea of what a good social contract was, and the man fixing to cook up Billy Come-Along and his mama had his idea of a good social contract. When these contracts came together, it was clear that every-body needed to understand where the others were coming from. The moral of this story is that you got to learn about life and whatever social contract you find yourself living in, or you're going to end up either dead, in hot water, or crawling along the bottom of life wishing you were doing better."

"Elijah, those three crabs were crabs!" I said. "I am not a crab."

"And you think that makes a difference?"

"All the difference in the world," I said.

"You think those crabs would think the same thing about you?" Elijah asked. "That life was different for them because they had the privilege of being crabs?"

"I think you just say funny things like that when you can't think of a good answer," I said.

"I'll finish up here later tonight," Elijah said. "Get your coat. I've got someone I need you to meet."

"So who is this guy again?" We had locked up the Soup Emporium and were going to see one of Elijah's friends at the fish market.

"I've known John Sunday a long, long time," Elijah said as we walked down Malcolm X Boulevard. "We met way back in 1981, when I was working at Macy's in the evenings. The night crew would order lunch around midnight, and John would deliver sandwiches and sodas. I lost touch with him for a while, but then I saw him selling fish in the market here about ten years ago. Interesting man, and an interesting part of the social contract."

I pictured a guy who looked like Elijah, but maybe a little bit older. He would be sitting between the stalls in the market talking to a group of students or reading from some old book that was written back before time began.

It was hot, and 125th Street was jumping. People had set up tables along the sidewalks and were selling books, DVDs, candles, and incense. Every other storefront had a different kind of music blasting out from loudspeakers, and some girls in tight dresses were dancing and showing off their stuff in front of the Apollo. For a moment I thought I saw my father looking at some shoes in a window. It wasn't him, of course, just some guy with the same build doing what he had liked to do, window-shop on 125th Street. The noise and the excitement of Harlem had always made him happy, even when he didn't have any money.

John Sunday was sitting on a folding chair in one of the rooms at La Marqueta. There were fresh fish in every booth, along with baskets of crabs, shrimp piled on ice, and lobsters on the long counter next to him. John himself was a big white man who looked like he had shrunk inside his clothes. They were just hanging loose on him. The stubble on his face made him seem almost gray, but his eyes, kind of pale blue, lit up when he saw Elijah. He smiled and pointed a bony finger at me.

"This your grandboy?" he asked Elijah. "He's tall enough to play basketball. You play any basketball?"

"I play some," I said.

"You got to watch old Elijah," John Sunday said. "He'll steal you blind. He just come around here to see me because he wants to steal one of my recipes. Ain't nobody can make mullet stew like John Sunday. Ain't that right, Elijah?"

"Sure is," Elijah said. "How you doing, John?"

"Doing good. Doing good. Sit yourself down," John said. He reached behind the counter and pulled out another folding chair and a milk crate. "Maybe I'll tell you some of my secrets."

We sat down, Elijah on the chair and me on the crate. It felt a little sticky, and I tried not to think about it.

"John Sunday, this is Mr. Paul DuPree, who is helping me over the summer," Elijah said.

I shook hands with John Sunday, and he had a good, firm grip.

"John came up from Shreveport, Louisiana," Elijah said. "Shreveport isn't a bad little town, but it isn't any paradise."

"You can say that again," John said, shaking his head. "My daddy worked in an icehouse in Shreveport, and so did my brother Billy. Billy was named after a famous preacher used to come around once in a while. We could hear him on the radio Sunday nights, too. When my daddy died right after the war, I went to work in the icehouse. I didn't go on the trucks, though. I'd stay inside all day, chopping ice into blocks for people to buy. Then, when it was time to go home, I'd go out and the hot air hit me and it was all about whew! And then some more whew!"

"It gets hot all over Louisiana," Elijah threw in.

"It ain't a bad heat because you don't have as many big buildings like they do in New York, so it cools off at night," John Sunday said. "But when you come out of that icehouse into that heat, it was like being hit in the face. More than one man caught pneumonia from doing that. You know a man's lungs can only take so much switching between hot and cold. Did you know that?"

"No, I didn't know that," I said. He was looking at me with his head turned to one side.

"Well, that's the truth," John Sunday said. "I worked for that icehouse from the time I was eleven until I was seventeen years of age. Worked like a dog, too. Work scares some people, but it don't scare me. I love to work, I truly do."

"Why did you leave?" Elijah asked.

"Get on, Elijah!" John Sunday pulled his head back, away from Elijah. "I told you I got that cooking job up in Baton Rouge. What's your name again, boy?"

"Paul DuPree," I said.

"Okay, I'm going to call you Paul," John Sunday said. "Well, Paul, a man come through Shreveport saying how he was going to go up to Baton Rouge and open him up a restaurant. He was looking for a cook and a waitress.

"Shoot, I didn't know nothing about no cooking, but I thought it was time for me and my girlfriend, Aimee, to get together proper and everything, and so when he asked me if I could cook, I said yes."

"And you couldn't cook?" I asked.

"I could cook some because I seen Miss Arlene, our colored gal, cooking, and sometimes she let me snap beans or do a few little things. Me and Aimee went up to Baton Rouge. I liked that town. Yeah, it was all right," John Sunday said. "And since that little restaurant was in the back of a general store over on the east side where they were doing a lot of building, we did some business. That's where I learned to make mullet stew.

"Look at Elijah looking over at me, hoping I drop the secrets of my stew," John Sunday said. "Man, if I give up these secrets to Elijah, he's liable to take them down on the Oprah show and make a million dollars!"

"And you would get half!" Elijah said.

"I'm waiting for Oprah to come on through here, and I'll get the million and then you get half, Elijah," John Sunday said.

"How long you stay in Baton Rouge?" Elijah asked.

"'Bout two or three years," John Sunday said. "Me and Aimee got together and had us two kids and then she got tired of everything and went back to Shreveport to live with her mama and made it clear that she didn't want no part of me. Said that as long as she was with me, she wasn't going to get nowhere in life. I guess she had read enough of them fancy magazines to want a big house and a shiny car or maybe a shiny house and a big car, I don't know. But the truth is that her name was Aimee Sunday and our two little children was John, Jr., and Palmer, and once a week she had to think about me whether she wanted to or not, cause I gave her my name, which was Sunday. Ain't that something?"

"Yeah, it is," Elijah said.

I could see that Elijah wanted me to hear John Sunday's story, but I didn't know why. It didn't sound like much to me.

"Then you were in the civil rights movement, weren't you?" Elijah went on.

"That wasn't no big deal. Some people say I was in it, but I don't say no such a thing. I did what I thought was decent and that's about it," John Sunday said. "'Lijah, you buying some fish?"

"Thinking about it," Elijah said. "How they look?"

"They looking good. Fresh as they want to be." John stopped and looked at his watch. "You fixing this for tomorrow?"

"You got it," Elijah said.

"Found a piece of job up in Montgomery changing tires," John Sunday said as he started picking out the red fish for Elijah. "It wasn't much, but it was honest. Then along came that bus boycott, and it was the stupidest thing you ever wanted to see. Lot of people was talking about how the black people wanted to sit up front and put the white people in the back. It wasn't about that. The black people said they would sit in the back, but when the bus filled up, they didn't want to have to get up and let a white person sit down. That was the unequal part of it.

"All the white people was getting mad. The bus didn't matter none, but everybody was talking about what was going to happen next. They was saying if you sat next to a black man today, the next day he would be doing something nasty to your daughter. Black people, they were walking into town to their jobs or getting rides the best they could. Some lost their jobs, too," John Sunday said. "You know, if you got a man by the throat, he can fight you for his life. You catch him by the job, ain't nothing much he can do about it.

"Anyway, some of the quality white folks would

go out and pick up the black people who worked for them. Some of the quality white ladies who had maids would go pick them up, too. Me, I was living just off downtown toward where the highway cut in, and I drove in to my job. Couple of boys lived near me and I seen them walking and told them to jump on in. I carried them in all through that strike. Lord, I got called all out my name behind that action right there.

"I was called a traitor to my race. I was called everything but a son of God. Didn't bother me none. People who want to hate you can find something in you they don't like. They have a talent for doing that. Well, maybe I'm lying a little bit. It did bother me some. What bothered me was that some of the people making the most noise had been raised up by black people.

"When the boycott was over and black people were sitting where they wanted on the buses, the whole thing looked a little foolish. Black people still couldn't ride the buses late at night in case some hooligans had more beer in their guts than they had sense in their heads and would mess with them, but more or less, things stayed calm until the March on Washington. Then it got real ugly.

"When I left Montgomery, I missed that tire-changing job because it paid good and you got good tips, but that town had enough ugly tucked up under its belly so that I didn't mind leaving at all. That whole thing in Montgomery made you start thinking and maybe listening to what the politicians were saying. I'm not a voting man, but if I was, I would have voted for Kennedy in 1964. Of course he was killed before he had a chance to run, but he was all right, even if he was a Catholic."

"You come to New York because you heard I was here," Elijah said.

"Come to New York because I heard you could find a job here in a heartbeat," John Sunday said. "I walked up to a man on Eighth Avenue and asked him where I could find a job. He looked at me like I was crazy, but another man, I think he was a Puerto Rican or something like that, told me to go over to Fifty-fourth Street and they had plenty of jobs over there. I went and found me a job as a deliveryman. That's when I met Elijah and taught him how to play checkers."

"You—you taught *me* how to play what?" Elijah was grinning.

"Elijah, you know you can't beat me in no check- ers," John Sunday said. "On the best day of your life, you could not beat me if I could get one eye open and move one finger to push the pieces around the board, and you know it!"

"If I had the time, I'd beat you two or three games today," Elijah said.

"If you had the time, I'd whip out my checker- board and whip you like a baby boy," John Sunday said. He had wrapped the fish in newspaper and was putting them in a cloth bag.

"I worked that delivery job at night, and then I got a little part-time messenger job in the daytime," John Sunday said. "I've always been lucky at finding things. I found that job in Montgomery when there wasn't a whole lot of jobs around, I found that delivery job and that messenger job, and then I found Jesus. All the time, He was sitting in my heart, waiting for me to recognize Him. When I did that, everything in life just seemed to be right. You know—what's your name again, boy?"

"Paul DuPree."

"I'm going to call you Paul," John Sunday said. "Paul, you know some people feel uncomfortable when I talk about Jesus? They don't feel uncomfortable when I talk about Obama or George Washington, but they get real edgy if I talk about Jesus. Ain't that something?"

"I know what you mean," I said.

"What I come to know was that my whole life was about Jesus," John Sunday said. "And when I got the feeling in my heart that He was there, it just made everything all right. Let me tell you—it made everything all right!"

"You made your peace with that landlord of yours?" Elijah asked. He was taking the money from his wallet to pay for the fish.

"Yeah, once I got the Section Eight papers filled out like you told me," John Sunday said. "You don't want no oysters?"

"Got some," Elijah said.

"Got them shucked and in a tub?" John Sunday said.

"Can't spend all day shucking oysters, John," Elijah answered.

"Can't play no checkers, can't cook, just what are you good for, anyway?"

"I'm good for a lot of things," Elijah said. "And you

know I'm experimenting with your mullet stew. I'm going to get it, and when I do, I'm going to invite you up to dinner. I'm not going to say a thing, either. I'm just going to sit back and watch you eat it. Then I'm going to whip out my ruler and measure the smile spreading across your face."

"Oysters in a tub?" John Sunday said. "I don't think so, 'Lijah."

"You don't have your scrapbook with you, do you?" Elijah said. "Mr. DuPree here hasn't seen anything like your scrapbook."

The shelf behind John Sunday was filled with sauces in bottles, containers of fish batter, and jars of seasoned salts. Under some bottles of tartar sauce was a big notebook. He pulled it out and handed it to me.

I thought it was going to be something on religion, but it wasn't. He had bought a regular composition book and filled it with page after page of magazine and newspaper articles about Paris Hilton. I looked through the scrapbook. There were pictures of Paris Hilton when she was a little girl, pictures of her with her family, and some pictures of her just about naked.

"I guess you like Paris Hilton," I said.

"I don't hate her, but I'm studying on her," John Sunday said. "I figure if I can find out what makes that little girl so famous, I will be the smartest man in the world. Just like some people study on butterflies or different types of roses, I study up on Paris Hilton. She gets on television and don't do much of nothing and everybody is falling all over her. But between me and Elijah, we will figure it out. Won't we, 'Lijah?"

"That we will, John Sunday," Elijah said. "That we will."

Elijah stood up and shook John Sunday's hand, and then the two men put their arms around each other for a few seconds before they said good-bye.

8

Me and Elijah started walking back uptown. All the way, he was showing me places he had lived or worked or where famous people had lived.

"Bumpy Johnson used to live over on this side of the street," he said, standing in front of a stand selling caps and cell phone chargers, "and Dutch Schultz used to have his office over on that side. You know who they were?"

"Guys dealing with the social contract?"

"Nope, hoodlums," Elijah said. "Bumpy was black and Dutch was white and they were both tough guys. That's when everybody was fighting over who was going to control the illegal gambling in Harlem."

"Who won?"

"The State of New York. They kicked out the

hoodlums and took over the betting themselves," Elijah said. "Only now they call it the lottery."

"Things are changing now," I said. "They're building up this neighborhood really fast."

"Harlem *is* changing," he said. "But Harlem has always been about change. We don't stand still up here. Only the image that people carry around with them stays in the same place."

Elijah is a slow talker but a pretty fast walker, and it took us twenty minutes to reach the Soup Emporium. When we got there, Elijah laid out the fish on the table and looked them over.

"Can John Sunday really cook?" I asked him.

"Yes, he can cook," Elijah said. "There's not much to cooking, Mr. DuPree. Just buy the best food you can afford and don't mess it up too much. People mess up their food by trying to do too much with it.

"He can play some checkers, too," Elijah went on. "He told you about his little jobs, but he didn't tell you nothing about how he used to hustle checkers over in Mount Morris Park—that's the one they renamed Marcus Garvey Park when they didn't have nothing better to do. Sometimes he used to go down to Greenwich Village and hustle checkers, but they got wise to him quick down there. He still beats them, but he loves to play the dumb old white boy who beats the city slicker."

"I got to go now," I said. "We have a game set up against some preppy dudes from Long Island who think they can play ball. I have to go down to Fourth Street and tear them up so bad, their arms will hurt when they even think of playing ball. That'll give you another day to give me an answer to my next question."

"What question will that be?" Elijah asked. He had already put water in one of the big pots to start cooking the fish.

"The question is, Why can't I live the way I've been living—not stealing anybody's ham sandwiches or anything like that—and not worry about your social contract?" I said. "You know some people who have heard of it, but I know a lot more who haven't, and they seem to be doing all right."

"*My* social contract?" Elijah shook his head. "Mr. DuPree, I have changed the soup I planned to have tomorrow so I could spend the afternoon answering your question. And now I have to spend the rest of my evening getting a new soup ready when I could be watching television with my feet up, and you tell me you didn't get the answer."

"What answer?" I asked. "You didn't mention the social contract all afternoon."

"I took you down to see John Sunday, didn't I? And what you saw in Johnny was a bright man with a good heart who lives like he wants to live."

"And?"

"I'm sure that John Sunday never heard of the social contract, and I'd be surprised if he's read an entire book in his life. *Any* book. But if you got about ten minutes to look at his life, you won't say anything more about not needing to know the social contract. You got ten minutes?"

"I got ten minutes," I said.

"Besides just getting along in the world with your fellow human beings, the social contract says how you can succeed in this society and how you can't. It says that our society won't let you succeed by robbing people. You got that?"

"Yeah, but I don't rob people," I said.

"You can't succeed by intimidating people, and for the most part, you can't succeed by going downtown and playing basketball against some other young men who think they can play. You still with me?"

"Go on."

"The social contract says you can make it if you have the tools that our society needs so that everybody is happy with you. So you need an education. You need to get some skills that you can take to the marketplace, and you need to understand enough about your assets to turn them into something you can get well paid for." Elijah said. "But John Sunday was bragging on how hard he's worked in his life, as if that was the only important thing. Hard work by itself isn't worth two cents on a rainy day if it doesn't give you a good life.

"When his wife left him, he thought she had gotten too many big dreams in her head. He didn't figure out that just because he was doing the best he could, it still might not have been enough to satisfy the needs of a family. I'm not saying she should have left him, but I can understand it.

"The social contract gave John a chance to have his voice heard, but he didn't vote. He didn't understand that what he did as a young boy, working hard but not getting an education, was going to affect him all his life. John has a good heart, and he's got more courage than most people, and he's trying to ignore the social contract. He's knocked around in little no-paying jobs all his life and still doesn't have a clue that the problem is not just him, and that there's something else going on.

"None of those jobs he had gave him a pension plan, and now he's in his eighties and he's still working in that fish market to make ends meet. I had to help him get welfare benefits so he wouldn't be homeless. He didn't have the information he needed to do it on his own. Now he's ending up being just like those crabs. Sitting on the sidelines, waiting for the water to get hot."

"You think that's fair?"

"It's fair, Mr. DuPree, but it's not easy," Elijah said. "Our social contract says that there shouldn't be anything blocking your way to the good life. But if you don't get up and get it or if you don't know what's out there to get, then that's your problem."

"I think that's wrong," I said.

"And if you feel something is wrong, you have to vote to put people into office who are going to give you a better deal," Elijah said. "But you need to know what they're talking about and figure out what that better deal is. John Sunday is a good man and a smart man in his way. But he's running outside the social contract, and he's not getting anywhere. There's nothing dumb about John Sunday, but he's never going to get much further than he is now."

"You also said the social contract protects people whether they know it or not," I said. "How come it's not protecting him?"

"It protects him against things that threaten the tribe," Elijah said. "Like crime, or an enemy invasion. It doesn't protect him against ignorance."

"And you're okay with that?"

"Mr. DuPree, I'm not always comfortable with it," Elijah said. "But if I truly believe that people are smart enough to learn and to take care of themselves, I have to accept it."

I left Elijah and started walking home. What Elijah was saying about John Sunday had me down. What I wanted was a system where everybody had enough to get by and could do their own thing. It didn't make a lot of difference to me that what Elijah said made sense. It wasn't fair and Elijah knew it wasn't, but he kept coming back to it like it was the only thing happening.

■ ■ ■

Just up the street, there was a fire and a car accident in front of the fast-food joint on Frederick Douglass. I went into the house, and Mom had made fried chicken and mashed potatoes.

"Are you learning to cook anything beside soup?" she asked.

"Not really," I said. "I can just change the amount of stuff I put in the soup and make stews, though. When it gets toward winter, I'll make some stews for you."

"When it gets toward winter, you'll be in school and finishing your college applications," Mom said.

"Hey, Mom, do you think Richard knew what he was doing?"

"Your father?"

"Yeah."

"What do you mean?"

"You think he had a plan for how his life was going and how he fit in and that kind of thing?" I asked.

"I don't know if he did or not. Half the time I don't even know what I'm doing," Mom said. "I go to work every day and try to do a good job. Then I come home and try to take care of the house. I don't do much else. I just try to do the right thing and work with what feels right for me to do. You know what I mean?"

I did, but it made me really sad. It didn't make me as sad about Mom because I thought she was doing all right, even though I knew her job at the clinic wasn't all that great. She liked it, though, and it was helping people and she was holding things together. But when I started thinking about my father, I wondered if he just didn't know enough about life to get over. If he didn't know, who was supposed to tell him?

I was close to being mad at Elijah. That was stupid, I knew, but I was still close to it.

It was hard getting to sleep. Real hard.

9

Saturday morning. I discovered Mom never really sleeps. I think what she does is to go into her bedroom every night and wait until I fall asleep and then assume her alternate identity as Alertia, the wonder girl. I had been out Friday night playing ball in Brooklyn with Terrell and some of the guys. When I hit the bed, I was exhausted and aching from being hacked. I had planned to sleep right through Saturday and get up sometime late Sunday night.

"Caroline's in town," Mom announced. "We've been invited to lunch."

"We going?"

"Yes. I haven't seen that girl for nearly a year," Mom went on. "Can you believe that?"

I could, and I did.

Caroline, Mom's older sister, had married and moved to Madison, Wisconsin, ten years ago. She used to call a lot at first, but then that kind of tailed off except for around the holidays. I knew she had a son who was older than me, but we had never hooked up in any serious way. Mom said that Caroline and Anthony were in New York for the weekend to go to some kind of film festival.

I didn't think Mom was going to be all that comfortable with the visit. She loved her sister, but Caroline's husband was a successful black doctor, and Mom's husband had been in jail for a good part of their marriage.

"The lunch is at twelve thirty," Mom said. "Why don't you wear your suit?"

"Because my suit is a fall and winter suit and it's too hot to wear it in the middle of summer," I said. "I'll wear my blazer."

"Does it need pressing?"

"No, Mom, it does not need pressing," I said.

I sat up in bed, and she was still in the doorway. "I'm so proud of you," she said.

Which meant that she thought I could hold my own when we went to lunch with her sister. It was all right with me. I figured I'd go to lunch, say something that sounded a little smart, chow down, and be out of there.

"When are they going back to Wisconsin?" I asked.

"They're flying in the morning," Mom answered. "Maybe the two of you can hang out when he starts at NYU?"

"Could be," I said.

When Mom left my room, I checked my finances and saw that I was looking good. Well, maybe not looking *good*, but heavy enough to carry lunch.

Mom fluttered around the house all morning, trying to figure out what she wanted to wear. She kept asking me what I thought of this blouse or dress, and I kept saying that anything she wore would look good to me. The thing was that Mom was still kind of fly and Caroline was definitely not fly, so that kind of evened things out between them. The other thing was that I didn't really care about Caroline since she hadn't come to my father's funeral. It wasn't a big thing, because my parents had been separated, but it was a family thing, and Caroline should have represented.

The lunch was downtown on Seventh Avenue at a Greek restaurant called Molyvos. We were supposed to be there at twelve thirty and showed up on the dot. Caroline and Anthony were already there and looking at menus.

"Caroline."

"Ebony."

"Look at you, girl!"

"You must be getting younger!"

"How did we let the time fly like this?"

"Time *will* fly!"

Kiss-kiss. Hug-hug.

Anthony and I shook hands, and we all sat down. A thin girl with dark hair and large dark eyes came over and took our drink orders. I ordered a Coke, Mom ordered a Diet Coke, and Caroline and Anthony both ordered sparkling water.

Anthony. My cousin was looking sharp. He was wearing a brown herringbone jacket with leather patches on the elbows, a light-blue shirt that might have been silk, and a yellow handkerchief that kind of just peeked out of the pocket. My man was GQing all the way.

"Anthony's been accepted into NYU's film school, and—oh, you tell them, Anthony," Aunt Caroline said.

"I've been considering careers in medicine and

film for the last several years," Anthony said, "Last year, I decided to do a few half-hour documentaries *just* to see how they came out. I had no idea of how powerful a statement a visually valid film could be. I had even less of an idea of how simple they were to produce."

"His father bought him a camera for his birthday," Caroline said.

"I completed a project, which I called, for better or worse, *The Juniper Song,* and it won some sort of prize, and I was offered a fellowship."

"That's wonderful!" Mom said.

"A lot of truly creditable filmmakers began here," Anthony went on. "We're here to see what the school has to offer."

"His father is still thinking he should become a doctor," Caroline said. "The camera was just a hobby."

What I noticed was that Anthony never looked me in the eyes. He was always looking off into space or at something he was holding in his hand. It wasn't a big deal, but it was as if nobody else was there except him.

Molyvos was a smoking restaurant. Everything was good. I had octopus for an appetizer just so I could tell Terrell about it, and then I had black risotto, just to get my funky thing on. The octopus, they called it oktapodi salata, was delicious. What made it even better was watching Mom watching me eat it.

Anthony ran his mouth all through lunch as if he was delivering a lecture or something. Their plan was really clear by the time the waiter took away the appetizer plates. Aunt Caroline, the doctor's wife, and Anthony, college senior and filmmaker, were breezing into town to see his flick at the NYU film festival, and Mom and I were supposed to fall out admiring both of them. Caroline flashed the tickets at us before putting them back into her purse. I wasn't impressed with Anthony, but I still wanted to check out his movie.

Caroline grabbed the check when it came and paid for it with a credit card. Mom wanted to pay our share, but Caroline just waved her hand as if the money didn't matter. I saw the bill, and it was just over a hundred bucks. Then we grabbed a cab down to New York University.

The film festival was held in the student center, and we found out that five short films were being shown.

The first film was by a French brother and sister,

and it was called *Friedrich and Elizabeth*. The whole film was about a guy sitting in a corner shouting about something and a girl on the other side of the room writing in a notebook. The film kept switching to an image of a gun, and after nearly ten minutes of the guy shouting, there was a loud *bang!* Then there was a picture of the guy lying on the ground and a picture of the girl stepping over his body and still writing in her notebook.

Anthony's film came on next. It started with a dark screen, then the sound of a clarinet playing a slow blues. I was impressed. Then the music grew soft, and we were looking down a narrow alley. At the end of the alley, there was something on the ground. It looked like a body. I recognized Anthony's voice as it came up.

"And Medea sprinkled powerful drugs over his eyes while she sang. . . ."

The image switched to a young white girl standing on a corner. Then the camera followed her into a hallway and onto the first-floor landing. She took down her pants, pulled out a hypodermic needle, and shot herself up. She was a druggie.

The camera stayed on her as she pulled up her

pants and went back out onto the street.

The next shot was of an older white guy, maybe nineteen or twenty, sitting in the park. He was talking about something he was calling the *Argonautica* or something like that, but he was slurring his words and you got the impression he was high. That was what the film was all about, this guy getting high and in between talking about gods and whatnot. It sounded as if he was heavy into Greek mythology.

A lot of the scenes were really hard to look at. The young girl and the guy were friends, apparently, and they both shot up. There was one light moment when they broke into a house and the girl fried some eggs up and they had breakfast together. What was funny about the scene was that the guy picked up a newspaper and started reading it as if he were in his own house having breakfast with his wife and not robbing someone's pad.

They lived in a basement. They had put a padlock on the door, and at night they locked themselves in. The movie ended when one morning he tries to wake her up and finds out that she's dead. The camera has him crying and holding her body for a while. But then he goes out, cops some dope, and shoots up.

Once he gets himself high, he goes to an alley, the same one that opens the flick, and falls asleep. The sound of the clarinet came up again, and the credits rolled.

Film by Anthony Rock
Directed by Anthony Rock
Photographed by Anthony Rock and Gino Colavita
Thanks to Gary H.
Thanks to Lavinia F. (1996–2011)

The film got a huge round of applause, but I didn't dig it. We watched the next three films, one of which was a cartoon, and then some school official invited us to the lounge to meet the filmmakers, who were all college students.

"Yo, Anthony, that girl really died?" I asked.

"Unfortunately, yes," he said.

There were easily a hundred people in the lounge, drinking wine or sodas, and I was ready to split. I told Mom and she said okay and apologized to her sister.

I don't know if Aunt Caroline was really on to the idea that we were leaving, she was so busy fluttering around Anthony.

"I think it was a very serious film," Mom said as we got on the uptown D train at West Fourth Street. "I think that any young person thinking about using drugs should see it and see what might happen to them."

I grunted and stretched my legs out in front of me. The train wasn't crowded, and we had found seats. I checked my watch and saw that it was only six p.m.

"I wonder where they got the money for the drugs," I said.

"Weren't they breaking into that one apartment?" Mom asked.

I nodded. What I was really wondering was if they had gotten any of the money from Anthony. People like him didn't have to worry about a social contract. They didn't have to figure out how their lives were going to go, just what paths they wanted to take. There was nothing in the film that said what he thought about either of the two druggies. They didn't even call each other by name. But for some reason they had let him hang around them and film them shooting up.

"You think that my father shot up like that?" I asked as we walked down the hill to our place. "In alleys and basements and places like that?"

"I don't want to think about that," Mom answered. "I really don't."

I could dig that, her not wanting to deal with my father's life. But I had to deal with it. I had to figure out who he was so I could give him a place in my mind.

10

Sometimes my thoughts wander and I don't know where I'm going. Or maybe I know where I'm going, but I'm not thinking about it and I just get there. That's what happened when I was going home and ran up on Sly.

"Hey, philosopher, where you going in such a big hurry?"

"Just chilling," I said. "Probably check out the baseball games on the tube."

"You in a big hurry to get upstairs?" Sly asked. He was leaning against the front door of his Bentley.

"No. I don't think so," I said.

"I got to make a run down to Thirty-second Street," Sly said. "Get in and go with me so I can see how much more you know about the social contract."

I wanted to say no real bad, but when Sly opened

the back door, I found myself getting in. Sly closed the door and got in the front passenger seat.

"This is my man Paul," Sly said. "What's your last name, Paul?"

"DuPree," I answered.

D-Boy grunted without looking around.

As D-Boy pulled away from the curb, the only thing I could think of was that they didn't have a real good reason to kill me.

"So what has the old man been teaching you?" Sly asked.

"He's talking about how the social contract is important for all of us to deal with," I said. "It's like rules that people have to follow if they want to get ahead."

"Follow the rules, follow the rules. That's what they used to tell the slaves. All you have to do is to follow the rules, and you'll be happy. Today when they talk about how we should all follow the rules, we hear people talking about crime," Sly said. "You know— 'Crime does not pay!'"

"He's talking about taking things from people," I said. "Like, if you had a ham sandwich, I'm not supposed to take yours and you're not supposed to take mine."

"Ham sandwich?" Sly looked back at me, peering over his glasses. "You serious?"

"Yeah."

"You remind me of Socrates," Sly said. "He lived in Greece way back when they were trying to figure out if calendars had to have numbers on them. He was teaching some half-ass radical stuff—like thinking for yourself—which their heavy hitters didn't like. They told him he had to stop teaching, and when he didn't, they told him he had to go. All his friends told him to split the city, but he said that wasn't right—he owed the government his loyalty, so he killed himself."

"Get out of here!"

"Yeah, he was an old fool," Sly said. "Fools commit suicide and think they're doing themselves a favor. That's why the old man is trying to brainwash you into his dog and pony show. Obedience first, then smile, then shuffle. Crime ain't about no damned ham sandwich. You ever hear of anybody going to jail over a ham sandwich?"

"Not really."

"You know what crime is?" We were making a left turn onto the West Side Highway. "Crime is a form of protest against the system. Sometimes it's the only path a poor man has. When the power structure and their flunkies—like Elijah—see that one of the lower classes is sneaking out, taking a different path than the one they laid out for him, they get upset and call that path a crime."

"Oh."

"You don't believe that, do you?"

"It's kind of hard to believe," I said.

"I didn't think you would," Sly said. "Sounds too simple, but you keep looking around you. Keep thinking about how the brothers are getting locked up and then ask yourself, What are they getting locked up for? Ask yourself if they were taking somebody's ham sandwich or just trying to get paid on a rainy day."

"There's a whole lot of ways of looking at things," I said.

"And it's human nature to find just as many ways of not looking at things," Sly said. "When most people run into a problem, the first thing they do is stuff cotton in their ears and close their eyes. Most of your life, that's what you're going to want to do, and most of the time, it's going to be *what* you do."

"You think that Elijah has his eyes closed?"

"He means well," Sly said, "but he's tap-dancing across a rainbow and telling the world that it's a bridge to the good life. It all sounds good, but it doesn't work for us. And when a young man like you comes along, somebody with something on the cap, we need to make sure that you're going to be useful to the tribe. We got enough nonthinking people running the streets, and enough of them behind bars or hooked up in the medicine business."

"Medicine?"

"I'm talking about all these guys standing on the corners feeling sick because they can't get around your professor's rules and start building something that looks like the American dream," Sly said. "When they get sick enough, they start self-medicating—smoking dip and snorting girl—to make themselves feel better or at least helping them get through the day. That's folk medicine. The man calls it addiction. What you call it?"

"I never thought about it as self . . . what did you say?"

"Self-medicating. People trying to ease the pain the system thinks they should bear."

I thought about the girl in Anthony's film and

wondered what pain she had been bearing. I wanted to think that my father had been in pain, too, and that he had been self-medicating, as Sly said.

We pulled up on a crowded part of Thirty-second Street, in front of a Korean restaurant, and Sly got out.

"Keep an eye on our passenger," he said through the window to D-Boy. "If he tries to steal anything, shoot him."

D-Boy had his eyes right on me in the rearview mirror. From the corner of my eye, I could see Sly going into the restaurant. Sly had a sense of humor, and he was smart, but he also acted like he wouldn't mind shooting you if he thought you needed it. A lot of brothers in the hood acted tough. It was a way that kept you out of trouble at times. If you acted soft, there was always somebody around ready to test you. But the stories about Sly made me think there was more to him than acting.

"You know I'm not going to steal anything," I said, throwing out my best smile to D-Boy.

D-Boy didn't say anything, but he kept his eyes on me. It wasn't a good feeling.

Sly was in the restaurant for five minutes or so.

When he got back into the car, he said that every-thing was cool, and D-Boy pulled off. I tried to think of something funny to say, but nothing came to mind.

On the way back uptown, Sly was quiet. I didn't know what he was thinking about, but I didn't want to jump in with anything stupid. I found myself breath-ing shallow so I wouldn't make much noise.

It didn't feel like we were going very fast, but we were passing cars on the highway. I noticed that D-Boy never said anything, but every once in a while he would kind of hunch his shoulders up and down. I wondered if he was carrying a gun.

When we got off the highway at 145th Street, D-Boy turned on the radio, and Sly immediately turned it off.

"I'm starting a new business on 145th Street," Sly said. "I'm importing goods from Korea and China and selling it wholesale from a store I'm opening. Anybody from the neighborhood who can prove where they live can get credit. I'm going to call the place The Woods. How you like that name?"

"I guess . . . it's okay."

"I'm calling it The Woods because back in slav-ery days, that's where we had to go to talk over our business and strategies. You like that?"

"Yeah."

"You're running scared, man," Sly said. "But you're smart. I'm going to need some smart people down the road to help me run the business. You think you might be interested?"

"You mean after college?"

"Whenever," Sly said. "People who can think don't come along every day. In the meanwhile, just stay strong."

"I'm doing it," I said.

I was halfway upstairs before I started breathing normally again.

11

"The best soup in the world is oyster gumbo," Paris B said. He was a big man who had worked in a hospital and was now retired. "You get you one of them big cans of oysters like the restaurants have and put them in some white wine over a little heat. Don't let it get too hot, because that'll toughen the oysters. Just warm them in that white wine for ten to fifteen minutes, so the oysters start to feeling good about theyselves. Then cut the heat and go back to cutting up your chicken parts, flour them down, and add some salt and pepper. Then dice some ham—make sure it's good ham—and fry that with the chicken until it's all nice and brown and your mouth starts feeling like it wants to smile but your lips is holding back."

"Go on." Elijah was sitting at the end of the table,

and I was sitting across from Paris B.

"Then you put in your water with some onions and a little cayenne pepper and salt if your pressure can take it," Paris B continued. "Let that cook for half the morning and then you add your oysters. Give it five minutes, then mix in your filé powder real smooth. Give it five minutes of some high heat and get your mouth ready for some goodness! What you think, Elijah? What you think?"

"I'm going to get Mr. DuPree here to start in on it tomorrow," Elijah said. "It's about time he had his own special soup. Every human being should have one somebody they can really love, and one soup they can make."

I liked soup, but I knew it wasn't going to make much of a difference in my life. On the other hand, I didn't know what I wanted to do for a living, which was sounding lamer and lamer to me. What I was seeing was that some people had clear choices about who they were, like Anthony and his mother. Other people didn't have clear choices and had to figure out what to do from day to day, like John Sunday, and maybe Lavinia, the girl in Anthony's film.

Sly was talking about a conspiracy, and I couldn't

go for that too tough, but he was heavy into it and could make it sound like the word. But I scoped that there were some thoughts waiting to be lined up and maybe I needed to get them together in a hurry.

When Paris B left, I swept up the dining room after I washed and racked the dishes. For some reason, Elijah put all the dishes in the closet every night. The next day I had to take them out of the closet and put them back on the table. One time I told him we could save time by leaving them in the rack. He thanked me and then put the dishes in the closet.

I was ready to go home when Elijah motioned for me to sit down. He asked me how my day off had gone, and I told him what Sly had said about how they make everything poor people do into a crime.

"Sometimes it seems that way," he said. "But you and me, we have to think harder than Mr. Sly is thinking, because he's looking out for himself and we want to think about the whole world. Thomas Hobbes came up with a system that he thought would benefit the whole world. You can look him up on the internet or, better still, you can get one of his books. John Locke was thinking about the world and various forms of government, too. So was Jean-Jacques

Rousseau. He wrote a book called *The Social Contract.* We've talked enough about the social contract for you to follow most of what he's saying. You have to remember that all of these authors published their books before the American Revolution, so Jefferson, Madison, Franklin, and Adams were probably familiar with their work as they hammered out our Constitution. If you read the Federalist Papers, and imagine the arguments that went on behind closed doors to inspire them, you can sense the same discussions about government, individual rights, and social relationships that the social contract theorists wrestled with."

"You read all of this stuff?"

"Yes, I have," Elijah said.

"Boring, right?"

"Do you think it was boring stuff to people who were going to become slaves or indentured servants, or have their land taken away from them?" Elijah asked. "And should it be boring to people who can't figure out a way of getting off the bottom of the social ladder? People like John Sunday?"

"No, it shouldn't."

"It's hard reading, but hard isn't bad if it's going to

make a difference in your life," Elijah said. "Thinking isn't bad, either. I think you know that by now."

"I got that covered," I said, feeling kind of confident.

"Okay, so we've covered two aspects of the social contract, natural liberty and civil liberty," Elijah said. "Now we're going to talk about a third aspect of the social contract—the fact that we are all living under some kind of contract—and then we're going to mix it up like a good soup with a strong stock of 'just the way we do things.'"

"Is this going to be confusing?"

"David Hume was an interesting thinker," Elijah went on. "What he thought was that there couldn't be a true social contract because a true consent of the people would involve everyone agreeing, and that never happens."

"Which is what Sly says," I pointed out.

"And there's enough truth in what all of these thinkers are saying for us to be paying close attention," Elijah said.

"And there's enough hurting to go around to everybody if you don't get it right," I said.

"Say that again?"

"You want to give me five reasons why I'm wrong, right?" I said.

"No, repeat what you said about the hurting, Mr. DuPree."

"I think there's enough hurting to go around if you don't get this whole thing down right," I said. "I mean, it doesn't have to be like a sharp pain or anything like that, but it could be just being miserable all the time."

"You couldn't have said it better, sir," Elijah said. "If you take it from Sly's point of view, they're hurting because there's a conspiracy."

"And if you take it from your point of view, they're hurting because they don't know about the social contract," I said.

"And if you take it from a conservative point of view, they're hurting because they won't follow the social contract," Elijah said. "But everyone is offering up some form of a social contract."

"So now you're saying I have to deal with it?"

"You can deal with it or ignore it," Elijah said. "That's up to you, but it's going to be there, and somehow the social contract is going to make your life better or worse. You think we can talk about it tomorrow?"

"Suppose I rupture my brain trying to get all this stuff in?" I asked.

"Then we'll replace your brain with the largest vidalia onion we can find and see if that makes a difference," Elijah said.

"Yo, Elijah, that's cold."

Mom and I watched the Yankees get wasted by the Red Sox. I thought of telling her what Sly had said about guys using drugs, that they were medicating themselves. It had made me feel a little better about my father, thinking he was trying to stop the hurt rather than just wanting to get high, but I thought I'd think on it some more before I ran it down to Mom.

12

"How's CeCe?" I asked. It was Friday morning, and Keisha was wearing cutoffs, a tank top, and sneakers.

"She's good. How you doing?"

"I'm okay," I said. "You been practicing your shot?"

"I took a hundred shots yesterday," she said. "Out of a hundred, I hit forty-nine."

"Yo, that's good!"

"How's that good when nobody's guarding me?" Keisha said. "You shooting from the three-point line and you get maybe two shots a game where someone isn't waving a hand in your face or going for the ball. I need to hit forty percent when I'm being guarded."

"So you can do it with time," I said. "We can set up the volleyball net and you can shoot over that. See how many shots you can make in three minutes."

"Let's do it."

We set up the volleyball net by putting one pole at the top of the key and slanting it so that it ran more or less parallel to the three-point line. I got three basketballs and passed the first one to Keisha.

Swish.

She had got the ball and went up instantly, shooting over the net. I passed the second ball, and she went up and nailed that one, too.

I threw her the third ball on a bounce while I scooped up the first two. That one banged off the rim, and I had to chase it.

The fourth ball fell through, and I knew the girl was getting her shot together.

The next ball rimmed the basket and came out.

Then I realized I had forgotten to check the time.

"Okay, let's start again," I said. "I forgot to time it."

"Those shots I made count!" Keisha said.

"Yeah, okay."

We practiced with the net for ten minutes, took a two-minute break, and went after it for another ten. Then we sat down, and I saw she wasn't even breathing hard.

"You're in good shape," I said.

"You mean after having a baby and everything?" Keisha asked.

"Just generally," I answered.

"Did you know that Wilma Rudolph won gold medals after she had her kids?" Keisha was wiping the sweat from her legs.

"You have nice legs," I said, instantly thinking I shouldn't have said it.

"Is that what you're thinking about me?" she asked. "Because if you're thinking you're going to get with me, you're wrong."

"Did I say anything like that?"

"So what *are* you thinking about me?"

"You're okay," I said. "I'm surprised you had a baby, but you're okay. At least you're trying to move on with your life and everything."

"And you think I shouldn't be trying to get on with my life?"

"Hey, I didn't say that!" I said. "I've just been thinking about how people move their lives along. You know what I mean? This guy I work for thinks we're all working under some kind of contract—the social contract—and I'm trying to figure out if that's right."

"A *what* contract?"

"An unwritten contract," I said. "It's like a set of rules everybody has to live by."

"And me having a baby broke the rules?"

"I didn't say that."

"You *insinuated* it, though."

"Yo, why you coming off so belligerent?" I asked. "You throwing everything I say back at me like you throwing rocks or something!"

"So me having a baby broke the rules?"

"Let's forget it, okay?"

"Why do I have to forget it?" Keisha asked. "Because you said so?"

"Okay, so you had a baby, that's your business," I said. "But in a way, that was breaking the rules, right?"

"Wrong, Mr. Mentor," Keisha said. "Because the rules don't work for everybody, and so they don't go for everybody."

"That's what I'm trying to figure out, if they work for everybody," I said.

"I just *told* you they don't work for everybody." Keisha was getting a little loud. "They didn't work for me. I started off like a good little kid trying to study hard and get good grades and sit up straight in school. And when I got home every day after school and heard all the fighting and cussing going on in my house, I couldn't remember a thing I learned in school. I couldn't do my homework because I didn't have a room of my own to do it in.

"So all that 'study hard and be good' didn't work for me. Maybe it works for you, but it didn't work for me. Then I started playing ball, and I put everything I had into ball because if I worked at it hard enough and played the game strong enough, I could shut out the other crap going on in my life. I was playing Little League baseball, then I played basketball, volleyball, and would have played football if they had let me. And I'm good at it, too."

"You are," I said.

"But then I got to be fourteen, and people started telling me that the rules changed and I had to start looking good and flirting with guys and going to parties and dances. That was the next set of rules. I met a guy who was like ten years older than me and he started calling me his wife and then I was pregnant and I guess I became his ex-wife at fifteen. That man didn't have no rules about who he was going to be with or when he was going to grab his hat and tip.

So the study rules weren't for me because too much shit was going on in my head, and then the girly rules weren't for me because I was just fifteen minutes of good times for some man who didn't need anything else. And guess what?"

"What?"

"I'm not going to have a good life," Keisha said. "I'm dreaming about playing basketball, but I don't think it's going to happen. Not really. So all your little rules don't mean diddly-squat to me."

"Then why are you here practicing your shot?"

"For the same reason I buy a lottery ticket every month," Keisha said. "Maybe a miracle will happen."

We didn't say anything else. When I looked at Keisha, she had a hard face on, but she was tearing up. I put my arm around her, and she leaned against me.

We sat for a while longer; then she got up and went over to where the basketballs were.

"You going to feed me?" she asked.

"Yeah." I got up and tossed her a ball. She shot it, a high arcing shot that fell cleanly through the net.

13

"When I was a boy, we used to use lard," Elijah said. I had picked up the ingredients he had listed, and he was watching me make soup. "Now we use butter or oil."

I was browning the chicken with the ham, garlic, and butter, and it was smelling good. When Elijah told me I was going to do the cooking, I was surprised, but I thought I was ready. I kept the pieces turning like he told me, but I was having trouble talking about the differences between soup and stew and pushing the pieces of chicken around in the pot at the same time.

"Don't let it burn," he said. "Burned meat never tastes good."

I finished browning the chicken and ham, added

the chopped parsley, salt, West Indian pepper, and thyme, and stirred it around the pot until Elijah signaled me to stop. The smells from the garlic and pepper and meat cooking filled the room.

"Now you have to add the stock and water," he said.

"How much stock and water should I add?"

"When does it stop being soup and start being stew?" Elijah asked.

I looked at him to see if he was kidding. He wasn't. I didn't know what to say, so I just shrugged.

"In my way of thinking, you need to have two and a half cups of liquid for each serving when you begin your soup," Elijah said. "If that cooks down to two cups per serving, you're just about right. Your friend Mr. Sly might think that less stock and more ingredients is better, and I don't dispute that for what he might be making. But Elijah is serving soup. Soup doesn't fit everybody's needs. Stew goes a lot further. I know that and you know that. But if I were making stew, I might run into a problem. Maybe I couldn't afford it five days a week. And if I did make stew, somebody out there would want dessert. Maybe they would want some rice to go with the stew. Maybe, even, they might want some soup to go with it."

"So what are you saying? Stew doesn't cut it?"

"No, what I'm saying is that people who come here benefit from my serving them soup. They get companionship, they get some good soup, they get some nourishment for their bodies, and they get something to do in the middle of the day. In other words, there is a benefit to a great number of people within my little social contract.

"Now, I only allow senior citizens to come here for soup. Some folks don't like that. They think I'm discriminating, and in a way, I am. In my soup emporium, I am the ruler. What I say goes. People who come here and enjoy the soup let me make the rules. I've been told that I should have the soup at a different time. I've been told I should have different soups."

"So you're saying you can't please everybody?"

"Some days I can't please anybody," Elijah said. "But they've given me the right to choose and they've given up their right to choose in my little kingdom here."

"I got you," I said. "They've made a contract with you to get the soup. Did you have a meeting or something?"

"What they probably did is the same thing the

cavemen did," Elijah said. "They looked around, saw something was working, and bought into it."

Elijah got up and turned down the heat under the large frying pan so that you could just see the flame.

"How come Sly doesn't buy into it?"

"Because man is a wonderful creature," Elijah said. "He's vain, he's cocky, he has a belief in himself so strong that he creates his God in his own image. Sly can see what I do, and he can see what benefit it brings. What he can't see is why he needs to limit himself to what an old man does in a small way. The best part of Sly is his wanting to be more than everybody else."

"The best part?"

"When ambition goes right, it's the soul of progress, Mr. DuPree. When it goes wrong, it can create all kinds of misery," Elijah said. "People like Sly start seeing their ambition as the purpose of life."

"You just think about that or you had it all figured out before?" I asked.

"I've been thinking for a few years, son," Elijah said. "A few years."

Some of the stock I was going to add was in the refrigerator and some, with the oysters, was on the stove. I put the chicken and ham and spices from the frying pan into one of Elijah's two big soup pots. Then I listened to him complaining that I should have put some of the stock in the frying pan and gotten all the bits from the meat cooking.

I cooked the chicken on high and had to add some water as it cooked down. Two hours later, I turned the heat down, took out the chicken parts, and forked the chicken off the bone.

"There's not much fat to skim on your broth, so your chickens must have been old," Elijah said.

"Yo, Elijah, we actually going to serve this today?"

"Either we do that or you stand up and tell everybody to go home," Elijah answered.

It was hard to fork the meat off the chicken bones because the chicken was really hot. But I got it off and into the main stockpot, and it was smelling even better. I was getting excited. It was like having a big basketball game for the championship, but nobody knew how I was getting ready for it.

Forty-five minutes before we opened the doors, Elijah had me add the oysters to the soup.

"You have to be gentle with them," he said.

I took some of the broth from the soup and put it

in a bowl to add the last of the spices. The filé powder had to be stirred as it mixed, and Elijah wanted it so there weren't any lumps.

"I can't see if there are lumps or not," I said.

"If you care enough, there won't be any lumps," Elijah said. "It'll be smooth."

I stirred steady until it seemed ready to me, then poured it into the soup pot. Taking the wooden spoon from Elijah, I stirred some more.

"Taste it," Elijah said.

To me, it was good. Maybe even great. I could hardly wait until the seniors arrived.

"I remember back in Wilmington, North Carolina, when shrimp gumbo saved a man's life," Sister Effie said.

"Ain't no gumbo saved no man's life!" Cranky old Mr. Peters turned his head and humphed. "That's just one of them stories that—"

"Do not tell me what I have seen with my own eyes, Mr. Robert Peters!"

"I know ain't no gumbo has saved a man's life!" Mr. Peters said.

"It was just past the Fourth of July, and this young

black man got into an argument with an old white man right there on Jackson Avenue," Sister Effie said, her soup spoon about six inches over her bowl of my soup. "The white man was a sheriff or something like that and was so mean he could look a hound dog in the eye and stop its heart. Anyway, Markie, that was the black boy's name, knocked him down and all the white people around that end of Wilmington was mad and they decided to hang that poor boy.

"His mama was real upset, and she didn't know what to do. She was praying and pleading and going on, but that didn't move the hearts of them white folks none. Then his aunt Carrie brought two bowls of gumbo to the jail, and she asked them to let him eat that bowl of gumbo before he passed on, and she put the other bowl down in front of the sheriff. The sheriff sat him down and watched as Markie started eating his gumbo. Well, when Markie had finished that bowl, it gave him so much life, he stood up and said, 'Come on and hang me!'

"That old sheriff came over and said he should have shot Markie and saved the rope from stretching. But Markie looked him right in the eye—you hear me? He looked him right in the eye and said he didn't give a damn, and that sheriff said he didn't give a damn either and he wouldn't even bother hanging him. And that's how that gumbo saved that boy's life."

"That gumbo didn't save that boy's life," Mr. Peters said. "They were always talking about lynching somebody down there, but once they got cooled off, they didn't bother none with it most of the time. That's what happened. Gumbo didn't save nothing!"

Everybody was enjoying themselves. I looked over at Elijah, and I could tell he was pleased with himself. His little piece of the social contract was working just fine. But what I liked mostly was that they were eating my soup the same as they ate the soup made by Elijah.

I didn't look into Elijah's face because I knew I would seem stupid grinning.

When everybody left, I asked Elijah if I could tell him about a girl I knew, and he said yes.

"On Fridays, I'm mentoring a girl," I said. "She's seventeen and she's had kind of a rough life. When she was young and going to school, her home life was so messed up she couldn't study. She got bad grades, and after that she got a baby, and I think—I know—she's pretty defensive. I'm mentoring her in basketball. She's a good ballplayer, but they're telling her she needs a three-point shot."

"Is that a metaphorical three?" Elijah asked. "I thought you only got two points for a basketball shot."

"Elijah, what world you living in, man?" I asked him. "They got a three-point line on the court, and if you shoot farther out than that line, you get three points!"

"I believe you," Elijah said, smiling. "Just checking."

"Anyway, I'm helping her with her outside shot, but she's so down on herself that I don't know if she's going to make it or not. She says the same thing that Sly says, except that she makes it personal. She says that the rules aren't for people like her, who have her kinds of problems."

"You believe that?" Elijah asked.

"I think I do," I said.

"When you first walked into this place, did you think you would be serving soup to senior citizens, soup that you made, and seeing the smiles on their faces?" Elijah asked.

"No."

"Mr. DuPree, I've told you this before," Elijah said. "But you and me and Sly and people like us have to think harder than people who give up and declare their lives are a failure or stop trying. Life is going to be harder for some people. It's going to be harder at different times in our lives. But if you're not ready to die today, then you're going to be responsible for tomorrow, whether you like it or not. You want to go home and think on that some?"

What I wanted from Elijah was a simple answer I didn't have to think about, but I knew he wasn't going for that. He expected more from me. I guess I expected more from me, too.

14

There was excitement on the block. Police cars blocking the intersections on both ends and a fire emergency truck parked in the middle. I saw Terrell, and he waved me over.

"They came down on your boy," he said, excited.

"Who?"

"Sly, that's who," Terrell said. "About umpteen dozen cops ran in that place he's opening. SWAT team dudes, some FBI guys, everybody. They were in there an hour and then they came out and started asking everybody questions about where they get their prescription drugs."

"Prescription drugs?"

"There's some kind of underground drug thing going on, and they thought Sly was in on it."

"They arrested him?"

"No, there he is, leaning up against his car with his arms folded."

I looked over toward the front of The Woods and Terrell was right—Sly was just leaning against the car.

We waited for almost forty-five minutes before the cops and firemen started leaving. Sly never moved.

"Whatever they were looking for, they probably didn't find it," Terrell said. "Unless you're hiding the goods. You got some prescription drugs on you?"

"You know I don't have any drugs on me," I said.

Miss Watkins came over to me and pulled my head down so she could whisper in my ear. "Elijah wants to see you," she said softly.

I asked Terrell to wait for me and went over to see what Elijah wanted.

"The senior grapevine has it that Mr. Sly is bringing in prescription drugs from Canada, Mexico, Korea, and India," Elijah said. "He's giving them away free to people who need them."

"To get high?"

"No, because they need them. He thinks he's providing a service to the people of the neighborhood,"

Elijah said. "The drugs are so expensive. But they didn't find any drugs in the place he's opening."

"Is that good or bad?"

"It's not in the social contract," Elijah said. "I can't tell you what to do about Sly, but you need to be careful. I don't want to say anything bad about him because I don't have the whole truth, but I want you to be careful."

I couldn't believe Sly would do something so out there. Or maybe I didn't want to believe it.

"Would you get pissed off if I told you what Sly says about you?" I asked.

"Go on, give me the bad news," Elijah said.

"He says you're tap-dancing on a rainbow and telling the world it's the bridge to the good life."

"He said that?" Elijah leaned back and folded his arms. "I like that, Mr. DuPree. I really do. He's right on the money, and I like the phrase 'tap-dancing on a rainbow.' The social contract has to be some person's or some group's ideals, their rainbow. Maybe if you and me and a hundred thousand other people make that rainbow strong enough, we can walk across it. What do you think?"

■ ■ ■

When I arrived at the Soup Emporium the next day, Elijah was frying up onions and spices.

"Black bean," he said. "You remember the spice that goes into the onions to add some depth to the soup?"

"Curry?"

"Cumin," Elijah said. "Is your head filled with Mr. Sly today?"

"Thinking about my father again," I said. "My mom put a picture of him and her on the mantle in our living room. He was standing with a beer in his hand. That's the only picture she has of them together. When he was alive, I didn't think about him much. He and my mom split, and he was either on the streets hustling or in jail. You know what I want?"

"To find a way to fit your father into the social contract," Elijah said. He turned the heat down under the pot, then poured in the stock and stirred it gently, the way he did. "And make him seem like he's not such a bad person."

"You're right," I said.

"Shortly before the Second World War, my father decided that he was going to make some extra money harvesting cane over in Louisiana," he said. "It was

153

winter—that's when they harvest cane—and my schooling time. He didn't care a bit for education. He had a habit of pushing his hat to the back of his head and spitting on the ground whenever he heard about a black man getting an education. I was about eleven, and the two of us took a freight train across the state to where they were hiring people to cut down the cane. Lord, that was some hard work, and I hated every minute of it and I was hating my father, too. Sometimes, when he wasn't around, I would push my hat to the back of my head the way he did and spit on the ground with just an image of him in my mind.

"But after he got tuberculosis and died, I started feeling different about him. From a distance, he didn't seem so bad. I wrestled for most of my young life over whether I hated that man or loved him. Isn't that something?"

"So what did you finally decide?"

"That life is like walking between two tall buildings on a tightrope. For some, the rope is wide enough and the walk is easy. For others, it's narrow and hard and maybe there's a strong wind blowing through their days," Elijah said. "But in the end, we learn we can forgive most people. The cushion of mortality makes their wrongdoing seem less dark, and whatever roads they traveled seem less foolhardy. In the end, I understood that I needed to make peace with his memory. As a thinker, though, I knew that if I was going to accept his humanity, the idea that he was more than an animal, I also had to accept him being accountable for his life."

"You think that's what I'm doing now?" I asked. "Trying to figure out if my father was responsible for his life?"

"You want me to run downtown to the easy answer store so I can answer that question?"

"Yes, I do, Mr. Elijah Jones," I said.

"I have some leftover beef trimmings I'm going to dice and put in the beans today," Elijah said. "If we dice them up fine, it'll add flavor but won't be too heavy."

"I got you, right?" I said. "You don't want to answer."

"I need you to find your answer, Mr. DuPree. I can give you mine and Sly can give you his, but you really need to work it out for yourself."

"I think that maybe there is no answer," I said. "Maybe this is just one of those questions that people like to argue about—like are the Red Sox better than the Yankees, or who should win the Oscars."

"My good friend—and he is my good friend—John Sunday hasn't figured it out, but I think you will. I think you will."

Elijah went back to his cooking, and I wondered whether he had changed his mind and was getting discouraged with me as far as the social contract was concerned. What really convinced me was when he took out something long and thick from the refrigerator that looked like a scallion and didn't get on my case when I didn't know what it was.

"It's a leek," he said.

"A *what*?"

"A leek," he said. "It rhymes with squeak. It looks like a large scallion, but understanding the difference in taste makes you a cook, not somebody just destroying good food."

"What's the difference?"

"A slight difference in taste, the way it flavors other foods, how many things you can do with it," Elijah said flatly. "You eat a thousand onions, then you eat a thousand leeks, and you got it."

"So you going to have this in one of the soups soon?" I asked.

"I was thinking about it," Elijah said. "Right now I'm trying to figure out what soup we're going to prepare for Mr. Sly when he comes here next week."

"Sly? Sly is coming here?" I looked at Elijah to see if he was kidding. What he was doing was peeling carrots. "Why?"

"I saw him on the street this morning," Elijah said. "And I asked him if he would like to come here one afternoon and present his case to some of the senior citizens, and he agreed."

"Why?"

"Because I believe in the wisdom that age brings sometimes," Elijah said. "I'd like to see how Sly deals with some of our people."

"And why would he show up?"

"Why would the great man show up at our humble abode?" Elijah looked up at me. "Great men like to make sure that they are really as great as they think they are. A great triumph is good, but a small triumph is very satisfying, too. It should be an interesting encounter."

I don't like confrontations with people, and I really didn't want to have one between Elijah and Sly. Sly was too cool to do anything stupid to Elijah, but

I didn't think Elijah could stand up to him. I liked Elijah a lot, but if somebody could be bigger than the social contract, it was Sly. Sly talked a good game about how the system worked against black people and poor people, but anybody could talk.

When I got home, Terrell called and asked me if I wanted to go out and get some pizza. I said I didn't and he asked me was it because of all the soup I was eating all day. I didn't know if it was or even if I ate that much soup during the day. Elijah had taught me to taste everything I was going to have other people tasting, so I never went home hungry.

"I got to ask you something about Keisha," Terrell said.

"What?"

"How's she doing?"

"Good," I answered. "I have her shooting threes over the volleyball nets, and she's hitting thirty-five to forty percent all the time."

"Yo, Paul, are you going to try to—you know—get with her?"

"No, I'm supposed be mentoring her," I said. "Not getting into her pants."

"Man, if I were you, I'd give it a try," Terrell said.

"It's not like you're taking her someplace she ain't been."

"Maybe I don't want to take her to someplace she's been," I said. "Maybe wherever she's been wasn't too cool. You think about that?"

"I guess," Terrell said. "You want to play some ball this weekend? I heard some guys were going to have a run out in Brooklyn this coming Saturday. Real early, though."

"I'm in," I said. "We'll hook up at my house."

"Got it!"

When Terrell hung up, I thought about the conversation and if I was scared to try to get with Keisha. Actually, I thought that Keisha liked me and thought I was somebody special. I didn't want to mess that up. I picked up the phone and called her.

"Hey, Paul, what's going on?"

"Did you mean what you were saying about my first step?" I asked. "You think it's too slow?"

"It's not too slow," Keisha said. "You don't *have* a first step."

"Keisha, that's cold."

"It's cold, Paul, but it'll make you free."

I didn't appreciate Keisha dissing my first step, but

I was beginning to like her a lot. I thought about what Terrell had said about getting with her, and I knew in my heart that things would change between us if I tried to mess with her. We were actually working out a little social contract just between the two of us.

I went back to the internet and started reading an article on the social contract by John Rawls. It was too hard for me to understand completely, but I saw he was dealing with the same ideas—what was justice all about and what was fairness all about—what me and Elijah and Sly were talking about, and that turned me on. There was a whole world out there of people thinking about things I hadn't known about just a few weeks before. I wondered what else was out there I should be knowing about.

Sly was supposed to come over in the afternoon, after the regular lunch. Elijah had invited five of the seniors over: Sister Effie, Miss Watkins, Paris B, John Sunday, and Miss Fennell. We planned to have the collard greens soup with white beans, a little ground chicken and garlic instead of ham, and loaves of black bread that a friend of Elijah's from a German bakery had donated. I noticed that the stock he was using was extra clear. I mentioned that to him, and he said he had skimmed it twice.

"Yo, Elijah, you nervous about Sly coming over?"

He always sat closer to the stove end of the table, and I sat either on the side or near the door when we made soup. He looked up at me and then looked away for a moment.

"If you are about ideas," he said, speaking slowly, "then you accept when someone challenges your ideas, but you don't want your ideas trampled. You want them to represent you well and you want to represent them well, too."

In other words, he was nervous.

The seniors showed up first. I had cleared away the bowls from the regular soup serving, and Elijah put out a fresh tablecloth and his fancy silverware. For some reason, I thought that Sly wouldn't show up, that he would send somebody over and say that he couldn't make it.

He made it. D-Boy came in with him, looked around the dining room, and then told Sly that he would be outside with the car.

"Good afternoon, ladies and gentlemen," Sly said as he sat down.

"Aren't you the young man that got that fancy car?" Sister Effie asked. "Blue or something like that?"

"Yes, ma'am."

"I bet you that thing cost you a lot of money!"

"It did." Sly smiled. I could see he was satisfied with himself.

Me and Elijah served the soup the way we always did and put the bread on a platter in the middle of the table. The conversation around the table started with the weather and what the president might do about social security, but the seniors were all peeping over at Sly. Everyone had heard about the police raid on his place and how cool he had been with it.

"This is a really nice place you have here, Mr. Jones," Sly said. "I see you've either preserved or remodeled the original woodwork."

"Most of it was in pretty good shape when I bought the place," Elijah said. "There were a few pieces of molding that needed replacing, but so many buildings were being modernized that it was easy to get replacement molding.

"And you can call me Elijah, if you will."

"And your soup is delicious," Sly said. "There's a Spanish restaurant on Twenty-third Street that makes a good collard greens and bean soup, but you've got them beat."

"Thank you, sir."

"So, from what you were telling me the other day," Sly said, "you were interested in me explaining why I didn't think much of the social contract. Would that be correct?"

"I'm open to anything you have to say, Mr. Norton," Elijah said. "I was just wondering how my friends here would see your argument."

"Well, sir, you have come to the conclusion that we are all involved in an agreement to help us get along with each other and help us prosper as a people," Sly said. "And to my best understanding, the agreement you're talking about is really just an agreement to keep poor people poor, hurt people hurt, and people on the bottom of our society from minding that they are down there on the bottom. And if you don't mind me calling you Elijah, I would appreciate if you call me by my street name, Sly."

"Sly? What kind of name is that for a grown man?" Miss Watkins asked.

"Ma'am, I can't help what people call me," Sly said. "But right now, I would rather get into Mr.—Elijah's social contract theory. I think it's mostly about theory and not what's happening here in America. Am I right on that?"

"Well, we can certainly talk about what's happening in America and we can talk about the Constitution as a model, if you'd like," Elijah said.

"Maybe I'm old-fashioned." Sly leaned back in his chair. "But I have a little problem with a piece of paper that's being held up as a model for everybody when it overlooked the fact that my people were slaves. I guess that doesn't bother you?"

"Son, have you noticed that you're free now?" Miss Watkins leaned forward over the table. "Or are them chains you wearing around your neck holding you down?"

"Lord, lord, I got a hanging jury here." Sly grinned.

"Sometimes a hanging jury will sharpen your argument," Elijah said.

"Just before they spring the trapdoor," Sly said. "But what do you say about those references to slavery in the Constitution, sir?"

"Well, they would have troubled me a great deal if I had been living in the 1700s or the first half of the 1800s," Elijah said. "And they trouble me now, when I think of how the compromises were formed to allow the existence of slavery when the founding fathers were proclaiming freedom and equality. But the Constitution is not just a piece of paper that we can look back on and say it's wrong here and it's wrong there. It's really a model of an ideal way of living, the best we can come up with. That ideal changed and grew as the country changed and grew. It's what we have now to hold on to and preserve as our basic rights."

"I think we can give Elijah an amen on that," Paris B said.

"He got my amen when he walked in the door," Sister Effie said, rolling her eyes at Sly.

"We got us a piece of paper, Elijah, and we hold it up for the world to see," Sly said. He was looking over the tops of his glasses. "But we're holding it up for the theoretical world—not the real world. We can argue about it in college classrooms, and in bars if we want to—"

"Elijah don't drink," John Sunday put in.

"Or dining rooms such as this fine establishment," Sly said. "But in the real world, aren't half of the people in this country still trying to prove they are at least three-fifths of a human being? Aren't we still running through the streets looking for the same freedom that our great-grandfathers were searching for? If you ask me, I think we can use an underground railroad today to get us out of the ghetto."

"Go on, boy, you can preach!" Miss Fennell said. "What church you belong to?"

"Right now I'm between churches, ma'am."

"Church never hurt anybody, Mr. Sly," Miss Fennell said. "You may be running around in the street, but God can still see your heart."

"Yes, ma'am."

"Umph!" This from Miss Fennell.

"Now, let me get this straight." Paris B dabbed at the corners of his mouth with his napkin. "Elijah, you want us to hear what Mr. Sly here was saying, and you and him don't agree on it. Is that right?"

"I just wanted to know what you thought of his arguments," Elijah said.

"And the debate is—as far as I'm concerned—does the social contract work for everybody, or does it keep certain people on top and the rest of us on the bottom?" Sly said.

"How are you on the bottom driving that big fancy car?" Sister Effie asked. "Or did you move the bottom somewhere from where you usually see it?"

"I'm not on the bottom because I don't follow the social contract," Sly said. "The social contract, according to our friend Elijah over here, says that I'm supposed to give up my rights as an individual to do whatever it is I need to do to get over, in return for what society is willing to hand over to me. I think poor people have been giving up too much and not getting anything back in return."

"Jesus said, 'Do unto others the same as you would have others do unto you,'" Miss Fennell said. "Is that the same as the social contract?"

"It's pretty close," Elijah said, "but I think Sly is talking more about our relationship with government, not the social contract in a strict sense. We hire our government—we don't have a contract with it."

"It amounts to the same thing," Sly said. "There are rules and laws that the people on top benefit from and the people on the bottom lose out on. If some banker gives you a shaky mortgage that puts money in his pocket and takes money out of your pocket, then that's all right. If a teenager takes money out of the banker's pocket, even a few dollars, he's going to jail. Do you think that's right?"

"They should both go to jail," John Sunday said.

"Now we are agreeing," Sly said.

"What's your answer to that, Elijah?" Paris B asked.

"I agree that the social contract that we have isn't perfect, and maybe it can never be perfect, but we need an ideal to live by," Elijah said. He was gesturing with his finger and he looked a little more confident. "If you have an ideal, something to hold your fellow men to, something that you can ground in law, then you have something that's precious. And when somebody tries to violate your rights, or take away your civil liberties, you have the privilege of righteous anger, and the assurance that in a fair legal system, you can do something about it."

"That's kind of like being married," Sister Effie said. "At least you have some rights and know a little about what to expect. These young people just living together don't have much to hold on to."

"I agree with that," Elijah continued. "And the social contract gives us a basic way of getting along with each other and making life enjoyable. Without some kind of a social contract—some agreement to examine and hammer into the shape that we need to extend the human dream—we'd be living the same way the animals live, by instinct and cunning. And I don't think that's the best that man has to offer."

"Now, what are we giving up again?" Sister Effie asked.

"The right to do anything we want to anybody we want," I said. "So you don't take my ham sandwich and I don't take yours. That way, we both can get along."

"Is this for old people or is it for everybody?" Sister Effie asked.

"Acting decent is for everybody," Miss Fennell said. "That's what it sounds like to me."

"But when you give up something, you need to get something back in return," Sly said. "What I'm asking is whether the people right here, around this table, are getting enough in return."

"In return for what?" John Sunday asked.

"I think he means for being decent and not taking somebody's sandwich," Miss Fennell said. "I think if everybody just acts decently, that's enough for me."

"Elijah, I was half ready for you today," Sly said. "I thought I was ready, but I see I was only half ready. I'm saying to you that this—and by 'this,' I mean the United States and the western world—is not the theoretical heaven you're painting it to be. And you're coming back to me by saying it doesn't have to be—the model is good enough. Am I right?"

"No, that model isn't good enough, sir," Elijah said. "But maybe, just maybe, the fight to build that model is the best thing that we have."

"Elijah got to get another amen behind that," Paris B said.

Sly looked down at his soup plate and then back up at Elijah. The corners of his mouth were tight, and I was getting a little nervous.

"What you got to say now?" Sister Effie asked. "You getting quiet all of a sudden?"

"No, ma'am," Sly said. "Just thinking. I have to ask Elijah one question, and I don't think he'll be able to answer it."

"Yeah, he can," Sister Effie said.

"Elijah, if this social contract you've been talking about is the salvation of the world," Sly said, leaning back in his chair, "why are black people still on the bottom of the ladder? We were on the bottom when this country was formed, and we are still scratching around in the mud trying to keep our bodies and souls together. And before you answer, I would like to point out what Karl Marx said. That as long as one class of people holds the keys to who works and how work gets done, they also hold the key to who succeeds and who don't succeed. To me, this is what's happening today, the same way it happened in 1789. We were slaves then and we aren't much removed from that state today. How do you explain that? Or do you just see black people as being inferior?"

"I see the struggle that you're pointing out," Elijah said. "I see the contending points, and I see that there's never a guarantee of fairness. But if you don't cope with the problem of the social contract, however it exists, you become a victim of whoever imposes their will on you."

"Man, you are slippery," Sly said. "You're placing all your bets on theory. I got to change the balance of this jury. Suppose all of you come over to my place next Wednesday for lunch."

"You have a restaurant?" Paris B asked.

"I'm opening up a new business down the street," Sly said. "It's not going to follow the social contract, and it's going to benefit a lot of neighborhood people. I'll cater lunch. Can you bring your people to my place, Elijah?"

"I think I'm obligated, sir," Elijah said. He was sounding confident.

"And I guess I lost this round of the debate," Sly said, standing.

"I don't know about that," Paris B said. "You had some good points, too. I'll have to be thinking about it. You both sound right."

"Well, I'm voting for Elijah!" Sister Effie said.

Before we left, Miss Watkins had two questions.

"Elijah, my pastor said that he couldn't win over all souls because not everybody wanted to go to heaven," she said. "If somebody don't want to go to heaven— all they want to do is drink and gamble and carry on like they're heathens or something—are they still part of this social contract business?"

"Yes, they are," Elijah said. "They aren't using it, but they're still part of it."

"And I would like to ask this question of our guest here," Miss Watkins said. "Does your mama call you Sly?"

"No, ma'am."

"I didn't think so."

As Elijah and I cleaned up, he was talking faster than he usually did. He was happy with the way the meeting had gone and was talking about how Sly was confusing government with the social contract.

"We hire or select our government to enforce the social contract," he was saying as he carefully folded the tablecloth. "It's the nature of all governments to try to take power from the people and keep it for themselves, but that's why we vote to change the government."

That sounded right, but like with most of what Elijah was saying, I would have to sit down with it and do some thinking. But what got to me most was Miss Watkins's question. What if everybody *didn't* want to go to heaven? She had put it in a negative way, that they were going around messing up their lives by doing bad things, but suppose they were more like John Sunday, doing what they thought were good things but just not understanding that it wasn't going to work for them in our society? Even if the social contract was made up by blind people who couldn't see where they were, so they made it up to be really fair, it wouldn't make any difference to some people. And if they truly didn't want to go to heaven, were they still accountable for their lives?

"Elijah?"

"Mr. DuPree?"

"I'm seeing some things that I didn't see before," I said.

"Like what?" he asked.

"When Miss Watkins was saying that everybody didn't want to go to heaven, I started dividing the seniors up in my mind. Some of the people, like Miss Fennell, just wanted everybody to act decently. I knew Sly wouldn't be happy with that, but I think John Sunday would have been."

"And what did you conclude from that?" Elijah asked.

"I don't have it all worked out yet," I said. "But I'm seeing how the contract is different if you're working it, or if you just let it work you. I still got a few problems with the details, but I think I'm on to something. Can you give me some time to think it through?"

"Mr. DuPree, I will give you as much time to *think* as God gives me breath to wait," Elijah said.

Sly's place, The Woods, had been a ninety-nine-cent store before he took it over. The walls were lined with shelves that had all kinds of goods on them. There were bins of clothes, all neatly wrapped in plastic bags, bins of books, iPods, and portable DVD players, and just about anything else you saw people selling on the street.

"The model is Indian," Sly said. "In India, they set up a series of microbusinesses supported by small loans. What I'm doing here is combining the two ideas. A brother or a sister can come in, establish their identity, and then we loan them the goods they need to set up a street business. We get paid back in cash after the sales are complete. So a man can start with zero capital, walk in at ten o'clock in the morning, and walk out in thirty minutes as a full-fledged businessman."

"Who's it for again?" Elijah asked.

"Anybody who walks in the door," Sly said. "They provide their ID, and we can deal."

I figured that was what Sly was doing downtown with the Koreans. They were importing the goods, and he was buying the stuff from them and using it in The Woods. The place was going to open up for business at three in the afternoon. Sly didn't mention anything about the medicines that people around the block were talking about.

D-Boy was sitting at a desk in one corner of the room, reading the *Amsterdam News*.

Sly put Elijah on one end of the table, and he sat on the other end. The same people who were at Elijah's for the first meeting were there: Paris B, Sister Effie, John Sunday, Miss Fennell, and Miss Watkins, and four people who Sly had invited.

The table was set up with fancy dishes with blue-birds on them, pitchers of water with lemon slices floating in them, and little bowls of sauces. There were salt and pepper shakers at either end of the table, and they matched the plates. I opened my napkin and saw that there was a red-and-gold border around the edges. The whole thing was really fancy. Some of the food was African, and Sly introduced the cook, a guy from Brooklyn.

"This is Brother Abou," he said. "I think you'll enjoy his food."

Brother Abou was heavy and dark skinned, and spoke with an accent. I thought he was either African or Haitian.

The menu was pan-seared chicken with peri-peri sauce, salmon and spinach with hollandaise sauce, and steaks with pepper and sautéed onions. I noticed that there wasn't any soup.

"You know, this food looks good, but it won't influence me one bit," Sister Effie said.

"It might get to me." Paris B was grinning all over himself.

I could tell that the seniors were feeling important that somebody was listening to their opinions. I liked it, too.

"I want you to meet some people from the neighborhood who you might not have met before," Sly said, holding his hand out to the people who were there when we arrived. "Why don't you introduce yourselves?"

"My name is George, George Pogue. I'm from around the way, 139th Street. I lived there most of my life." The guy was small and thin, and didn't have many teeth. "Sly asked us to tell our stories, so I'll begin with mine.

"I went to Lane in Brooklyn and I did okay, but then I ran into the drug scene. I got busted when I was eighteen for dealing and did sixty-four months on an eight-year bid, and then when I got out, I ran into an aggravated assault charge and I got twelve years on that, plus four for illegal possession of the gun. So, all in all, I did eighteen years in the slam, which is just a little more than half my age."

"So half your life you've been in prison?" Sly asked.

"Yeah. I'm trying to stay straight now, but there's no jobs out here and I don't know how people expect me to live," George said.

"Go on, Nestor." Sly nodded toward the guy who looked Spanish.

"Same old, same old," Nestor said. "I left school early, got into this little street hustle and that little street hustle until I got caught up in drugs. Armed robbery, possession with intent to distribute, aggravated this and aggravated that, it all amounted to seventeen years. I didn't actually hurt nobody except myself."

"You didn't think taking drugs was wrong?" Miss Watkins asked.

"I knew it was against the law," Nestor said. "I'm not going to lie about that. And even if it wasn't against the law, I knew it was foul. But when I was dibbing and dabbing and got caught up, I couldn't get no help. They would run—what were they doing then? Methadone. But that just cuts down what you need to get you through the day. It don't take the weight off your life. You know what I mean?"

"And you never heard anything about drugs until you—what did you say?—started dibbing and what-not?" Miss Watkins had her head turned so her chin pointed at Nestor.

"Yeah, I heard"—Nestor glanced toward Sly— "but a lot of people make mistakes. I guess I'm not perfect."

"Johnnie?" Sly nodded toward the woman. She was cute, with short, neat hair and small gold ear-rings. I wondered if she was Sly's girlfriend.

"My name is Johnnie Mae Stokes. I've never been in jail and I'm afraid of drugs," Johnnie said. "My story is nothing special. I was with a man and we had two children together. Then he got locked up for breaking and entering. We weren't married. Then I had two more children before I had my tubes tied. Right now I'm on welfare, as Sly knows. Sometimes I get some work cleaning houses, but most of the time, I don't have anything to do. I'm not good with numbers or anything like that, and I can't type, so there's really nothing out there for me. My two youngest children are four and six. They can't take care of themselves, and if I get a babysitter, it'll cost me more than I'm making. I think I made mistakes, but, you know, I'm human."

As Abou took our lunch orders, it came to me that all the people on Sly's side of the table were going in the same direction: that there was nothing they could do to change their lives.

I ordered the chicken and an iced tea. I wished I had a notebook so I could take down some of the things that Sly's people were saying. I tried to imagine them, sitting around with their ham sandwiches tucked under one arm. That was funny at first, but it didn't seem funny when I realized that they had been sitting outside the social contract when they made their "mistakes," and they were still looking at themselves the same way.

"Okay, this is my man Binky," Sly said, putting down his menu. "Binky, I want you to tell them how your arrest went down. The whole story."

"I was going to George Washington High and I was doing good . . . I mean well," Binky said. He looked to be a few years older than me. "I wanted to be either an engineer, because I've got an uncle who's an engineer, or a time-study guy, because my cousin does that and it sounded good. My father works in the post office, which isn't bad, but I didn't go for that too tough.

"Anyway, everybody in my family thought I was going to be something special, and that made me feel good because I believed it, too. I had a hobby, which was martial arts. I took judo and karate at the Y on 135th Street. Some of the other things we learned was how to use swords and stuff. It really wasn't swords, it was bamboo sticks. And all of us practiced with chukka sticks—that's two sticks with a chain or a rope connecting them.

"You can hurt people with those things," Paris B said.

"With two sticks and a chain?" John Sunday asked. "How you going to hurt somebody with two sticks and a chain?"

"You can mess somebody up pretty bad if you know how to use them," Binky said. "Anyway, one day I was coming home from school, and around 137th Street, a fight broke out between some brothers and some white kids who went to City College. Me and my boy, a guy named Frankie, crossed the street because we didn't want to get mixed up in it. It wasn't like a war or nothing, just some fists, from what we could see.

"So we watched from across the street for a minute and then started on home. We were three blocks away and our minds were on something else when all of a sudden this car pulls up alongside us and these two white guys hop out. They're cops, and they ask us if we were involved in the fight. I said no and Frankie said no and then they looked into our backpacks and found my chukka sticks. I didn't know they were illegal, and when the dude down at the station started talking about a fourth-degree felony, I thought he was kidding.

"Some college guy had gotten his nose broken and two teeth knocked out in the fight, and they were looking to see who had done it. I heard that somebody had a bat or something like that, but when they found the chukka sticks, they said I might have done it. They couldn't prove it, but they still had me for possession and I got eighteen months in juvenile."

"Okay, Elijah, what I'm going to ask you to do," Sly said, "is weigh in with your theory about the social contract and put it up against these brothers and this sister who have to face life without benefit of your protective theory."

"I can see where the men using drugs would have a hard time," Paris B said. "But I know what chukka sticks are, and I didn't know they were illegal. I sure didn't know you could get jail time for that. That don't seem right to me."

Mr. Abou brought out salads for everybody. The salad looked good, but I was more interested in sneaking a glance over at Elijah, to see what he was going to say.

Elijah's face was working, like he was thinking real hard but hadn't got to the point where the words were actually coming out yet.

"If you knew that drugs were illegal, why did you choose to use them?" Miss Fennell asked.

"I knew I was wrong," George said. "But I didn't think I was half my damn life wrong. People out here killing people or robbing millions of dollars don't spend half their lives in no jail. I'm not saying I was correct, but what I'm asking is, just how wrong was I?"

"And I don't think I was wrong to have sex four times," Johnnie Mae said. "Most people have sex at least four times in their lives. And if my man had been together, I could be home watching Oprah in the daytime and buying stuff on the Home Shopping Network. Now my job—and it's a j-o-b, honey—is trying to survive and raise my children on welfare."

"So, Elijah." Sly folded his hands in front of himself as if he was going to pray or something. "Here we have a small gathering of people who have had a range of experiences. Some of them have spent years in either jail or the prison of poverty. Johnnie Mae is living in a society that offers her little hope of getting ahead and little hope of finding her way into that door that is marked AMERICAN DREAM. And it seems to me that your social contract theory works against them. Not for them. And the greater good that you spoke about the other day scoots past these brothers and this sister and leaves them permanently in a kind of limbo. So what good is the social contract?"

"Sly, you want a simple answer, and the truth is that there isn't one," Elijah said. "But let me break it down as much as I can to a few points."

"Go on, Elijah," Sister Effie said. She was leaning forward in her chair.

"The social contract protects these people as much as it does me, or anyone here," he said. "It guarantees their fundamental rights—"

"The right to be poor and suffering in the richest country on earth?" Sly asked.

"The right to be poor and suffering in the richest country on earth, but free and with the hope of doing better," Elijah said.

"So if there aren't any jobs out here—and there aren't," Sly said, "then they are reduced to being semislaves. We don't have to worry about the horrors of slavery because they aren't official slaves, just sort of semislaves. And if the government, in its quest for the greater good, decided not to give Johnnie Mae food stamps, she might have to sell her body to whoever bid for it on the street to feed her children. But she would have hope while she did it, wouldn't she?"

"Individual stories don't change the whole," Elijah

said. "And it's the whole that holds the promise for these young people. They see this is a rich society, the same as you do. And they want to be part of it. But they've gone off course—"

"That's the truth," Sister Effie said.

"So Binky went off course when he was trying to keep his nose clean and do the right thing, and now he's got a record," Sly said. "Plus he had the humiliating experience that one out of every four young black men has, of being locked up like an animal and treated like an animal, in your social contract system. That could affect his whole life, and you say it's all right because of some vague sense of a whole system."

"I didn't say it was all right," Elijah said. "I said a system exists, and it's not perfect. It can't be perfect because it's put in place by human beings."

"I don't see you suffering too much, Mr. Sly," Sister Effie said.

"That's because I've turned my back on the social contract, sister," Sly said. "Because I recognize it as what it is for a poor man—volunteer slavery."

Sly could run his mouth. He had his arguments down, and they were good. And the people Sly had brought along sounded convincing. They didn't look like bad people. They were as ordinary looking as anybody you saw on the street.

The conversation kind of died down for a while, and then Paris B started talking about the food and everybody said how good it was. Sly said he was thinking of opening up a restaurant in Harlem.

Even though we had stopped discussing the social contract, it was on everybody's mind. I watched Binky and Johnnie Mae talking. They seemed to be having a good time. George was checking his watch, and I wondered if he was thinking about selling drugs or something.

"Honey, can I ask you a question?" Miss Watkins again. She had reached over and put her hand on George's arm. "When you were out there using them drugs, did you know they were messing your life up?"

"I did to an extent, but I didn't see no doomsday on the horizon. You know what I mean?" George said. "I could handle my weight, but what the justice system threw down on me snatched away my whole life."

"According to Mr. Sly over here, drug people don't have to be thinking about going to jail or anything like that," Sister Effie said. "Isn't that what you're saying, Mr. Sly?"

"He shouldn't have to, and he wouldn't have to if the social contract was fair," Sly said. "But I don't see any fairness in condemning a young man for life because he's made a mistake that didn't hurt anybody but himself. And I don't see slamming Johnnie's children because of the ups and downs of her life."

"Yo, Sly, I'm seeing something different here," I said.

"Run it, youngblood!"

"Okay, so what I'm seeing is that the social contract is out there, and you either deal with it or you don't," I said. "If you don't, then whatever happens, *happens*! It's as if you become a universal victim. Anything that comes your way can mess with you. It's almost as if you're in the middle of the street and there's a gang war going on. Bullets flying everywhere, and you're just standing in the middle of the street hoping nothing hits your butt.

"My man over there said he knew drugs were illegal, but he jumped into that scene and took his chances and lost," I said. "Nestor hooked up into the same scene and yes, you can criticize it, throw rocks at it if you want, but he knew the program, so him saying that he's been kicked around is right, but did he really expect everyone to stand up and give him a hand for breaking the law?"

"You're strong, but you're wrong, my brother," Sly said. "For Nestor to follow the social contract that Elijah is running, he has to have the same incentives, and the same opportunities as that dude down on Wall Street making millions of dollars a year and looking down his nose at people in this neighborhood. Or are you saying that people who live in Harlem are supposed to be getting their butts kicked?"

"You have to give him credit for being a man," I said. "And along with that credit comes the duty to step up and get in the game. He may not have the best first step in the world, but he's still got to deal."

"I'm dealing, my brother!" Nestor raised his voice.

"Oh, what you doing, baby?" Miss Watkins asked.

"And wasn't the social contract there for all of these young people?" Elijah asked. "Could they have used it to their advantage?"

"What contract he talking about, Sly?" Nestor asked. He had a piece of chicken in his hand and pointed toward Elijah with it.

"He's talking about a theoretical contract between the people and the government that is supposed to be for everybody's benefit," Sly said. "Me and the brother at the other end of the table are disagreeing about whether the contract is really benefiting poor people or just keeping them poor."

Sister Effie said we should have a vote, and I knew she was ready to vote for Elijah again. The thing that came to my mind right away was that if you thought you didn't have to deal with the social contract, whether it was good or bad, you were going to have a problem. In fact, you were going to be a victim of whatever came your way.

We were getting ready to vote again, but it never happened.

Paris B was explaining to Sly's friends how we had voted at the Soup Emporium and how Elijah had won, and I was mentally counting how many votes Sly and Elijah would get this time around, when the door crashed open.

BLAM!

Everybody jumped. We turned and looked toward the door and saw two big dudes come busting into the room.

"Where's Sly?" The guy was wearing dreads, a painted denim jacket, and black pants.

"We're not open until later this afternoon," Sly said, standing. "Now if you'll just be so kind as to take your ass on out of here—"

"I ain't going nowhere, punk!" Dreads opened his jacket, and I could see he was cut. "I came here yesterday to get some goods, and your flunkies talking about all I can get is what I can carry in a damned garbage bag."

"Yo, man, I asked you politely to catch the other side of the door!" Sly was pissed.

"I told you I ain't going nowhere until I get what I need," Dreads said, coming toward where the table was set up. "I think you're just fronting for the white man, anyway. You trying to keep the *people* down and yourself on top!"

"Lord, don't shoot nobody!" Sister Effie called out.

I turned and saw D-Boy coming across the room with an Uzi in his hand, shoulder high, pointed right at Dreads. Dreads turned and saw the gun and threw both hands up.

What happened next was scary. I watched as Sly tried to hold down his temper. He was light enough so we could see him turn red and then go pale.

Sister Effie was shaking her head and John Sunday was halfway crouched over, as if he was ready to dive under the table.

Dreads and his buddy left in a hurry. D-Boy put down the Uzi, grabbed his jacket, and left. I didn't know what he was going to do outside, but I was glad it wasn't aimed at me, whatever it was.

16

I felt excited on my way to the Soup Emporium. I wanted to tell Elijah what I had figured out about the social contract, about how it was different for people who were active and those who weren't. He might have wanted to talk about Sly and D-Boy and the Uzi, and I promised myself I would hold off until he finished what he had to say about that scene.

On the block, there was an argument between some guys on a street-cleaning truck and a brother who didn't want them throwing dirt on his machine.

"You don't clean worth a damn, anyway," the brother was saying. "All you doing is spreading the dirt around and kicking up germs in the air!"

"We'll give you a ticket for interfering with our job," the street cleaner said.

Too much. I ducked into Elijah's, hung up my jacket, and started washing up.

"How you doing?" I asked.

"Still here," Elijah said. "What kind of soup you thinking about making today?"

"You want to go with the collard greens and ham?"

"You buy collard greens?"

"No."

"So what kind of soup you thinking about making today?"

I looked in the vegetable bin and saw we had potatoes, celery, carrots, and green peppers. In the refrigerator, we had frozen smoked neck bones, ham hocks, and chicken breasts, plus a bag of bones for stock.

"What are you thinking about?" I asked. Just then the doorbell rang. "I could go buy some collard greens if you wanted me to," I said as I started toward the door.

It was a little after eight, and sometimes the guy who reads the meter came that early, and I was going over in my head what we needed for collard greens and ham soup. It wasn't the meter reader. It was Keisha.

"I called your mother and she gave me the address," she said. She was holding CeCe on her hip.

"What's up?"

"Can I come in?"

"Yeah, I guess," I answered.

Keisha walked inside and started looking around the Soup Emporium. I motioned for her to go into the kitchen. Elijah looked up.

"Elijah, this is Keisha Marant," I said. "She's the one I'm mentoring in basketball on Fridays."

"How do you do?" Elijah stood up and nodded his head toward Keisha.

"Keisha, this is Elijah Jones, and he runs this soup emporium," I went on. "We serve soup—real good soup to senior citizens, five days a week."

"That's sweet," Keisha said. "I like soup."

"Mr. DuPree is just trying to decide what soup we're going to have today," Elijah said.

"I can't stay," Keisha said. "I just wanted to come by and tell you face-to-face that I won't be coming on Fridays anymore."

"Why are you quitting now?" I asked. "I thought you needed to work on your shot."

"It doesn't make that much difference," Keisha

said. CeCe was trying to put her fingers in Keisha's hair, and she put her daughter on the floor.

"Either they take me with the game I got or they won't take me. I can only be who I am."

"What's the problem with your game?" Elijah asked.

"Keisha is quick and aggressive," I said. "Which is good, but one coach said that if she had a better outside shot, she would be more effective."

"Give the opposing player something else to think about," Elijah said.

"You know basketball?" Keisha asked.

"Not really," Elijah said. "But it does make sense, doesn't it?"

"A lot of things make sense," Keisha said. "But I'm not going to do them all."

"Besides making soup, we also spend a lot of time discussing the social contract," Elijah said. "Have you ever spoken to Paul about that?"

"He tried to run it past me," Keisha said. "I don't think he knows too much about it."

"Yo, Keisha! Lighten up! I know more about it than you do!" I said.

"Who cares?" Keisha said. CeCe had put her arms

around her mother's legs, and Keisha was rubbing the little girl's back. "Look, I've got to split. I think I can cop a job for the rest of the summer, and I can definitely use the money."

"You should care, if you have a little girl," I said.

"So run it, fool," Keisha said.

"The social contract is an agreement between people and between the people and their government for everybody's mutual benefit," I said.

"That doesn't mean a thing to me," Keisha said. "And I can lay that on CeCe all day and it won't mean a thing to her, either."

"Okay, I got another way of looking at it," I said. "Say there's a track that runs from here to the Harlem Children's Zone on 125th Street, okay?"

"I know where it is," Keisha said.

"And somebody told you that if you went along that track, you'd get a free dinner for the rest of the week for you and your daughter, okay?"

"Go ahead."

"And as you walked along the track, you saw some people running by you, and some roller skating by you, and some just playing cards along the way," I said.

"Which is what you see if you walked down there from here," Keisha said.

"But then, when you got to 125th Street, they handed you seven peanut butter and jelly sandwiches and said, 'That's your free dinners,'" I said. "How would you feel?"

"I'd feel mad," Keisha said.

"Especially when you saw that the people who got there first were getting coupons to have dinner at a fancy restaurant. And when you asked the people why you were only getting peanut butter and jelly sandwiches, they told you that you lost the race and that's all the losers get."

"They should have said it was a race in the first place," Keisha said.

"That's what the social contract is about, letting everybody know what's going down," I said. "Now, if they told you that if you came to Elijah's Soup Emporium, you were going to get some money, you would be thinking you needed to know if it was a race or not, right?"

"Go on." Keisha sat down and pulled CeCe up on her lap.

"But you see that everybody else knows it's a race,

too." I said. "But the ones who got there first also got bicycles to come back uptown."

"Okay, so I ran into a foul situation," Keisha said. "I would just leave it alone and go about my business."

"What I'm saying about the social contract is that you're in it now," I said. "And you can't walk away from it. You're in a race that has rules and has rewards for people who know those rules and know how to deal with them well. The people who started out knowing it was a race have a big head start on you, and they're going to get theirs no matter what you do."

"You buying this?" Keisha turned to Elijah.

"I'm buying it because I believe that what Mr. DuPree is saying is true," Elijah said. "There are agreements, written and unwritten, that determine how we live, to a large extent."

"Okay, so from the get-go . . . you think if I go down to 125th Street and *after* I get down there they tell me I was in a race—*after* I get down there they tell me—that I was being treated fair?" Keisha asked.

"Yo, mama, I didn't say it was fair—" I started.

"I'm not your mama," Keisha interrupted. "And just run it down—is that fair or not?"

"It's not fair, but it's real," I said.

"Go on. . . ." Keisha was looking at me sideways.

"So what I'm saying is that if you want to hook CeCe up, you got to school her on what's going on. She has to know she's in a race, she has to know what the rules are, and she has to learn to deal."

"And who is making these rules and setting up this race?" Keisha asked.

"People who make the laws," I said. "The government, sometimes. Special interest groups. People on the top."

"I never heard of this crap before I met you, Paul."

"And when you were coming downtown the first time and saw people sitting on the side of the road playing cards and not even in the race, you know they haven't heard of it, either."

Keisha turned to Elijah. "Don't we have a Constitution that says everything is supposed to be fair?"

"Mr. DuPree?"

"It's fair under some conditions," I said. "If you know what's going down, and have the wheels to deal, then it's just about fair. If you don't know what's going down, or if you think you can skate by, or if you mess up and break one of the big rules, then you have a problem."

"Like having a baby?" Keisha asked, pulling CeCe closer to her.

"Like not realizing what you need to do for your baby," I said. "If you got it going on, then CeCe should have it even better than you."

"And is that what you guys sit up here and talk about every day?" Keisha asked.

"Quite a lot of the time," Elijah said.

"So how is CeCe going to get all of this when I don't even know it?" Keisha asked. "There's stuff out there that—ways of getting over—that I can't get next to, and you're saying I have to know it to pass it on to my daughter?"

"You kind of know it now," I said. "You see things going on. You see people who aren't doing anything with their lives—"

"Watching the world go by."

"Watching the world go by and becoming victims of anything that comes their way. You see it, and that's why you're out there practicing that outside shot. You're aiming yourself for college because you know that's a better way."

"I don't even care about myself," Keisha said. "I just want CeCe to have all the right stuff so she can do well."

"How old is your daughter?" Elijah asked. "She's really lovely."

"Going on two." Keisha's face softened. "If Michelle Obama doesn't run, CeCe'll be the first black woman president."

CeCe made a sound that could have been "president" and stuck her chin up in the air. She was as pretty as Elijah said she was, and even prettier when responding to Keisha.

"I got to be going," Keisha announced. "I guess I'll see you Friday, Paul. And you'd better be thinking about my three-point shot between now and then."

"I'll have it locked up," I said.

Keisha picked CeCe up with one hand and put her back on her hip.

"Good-bye." Elijah waved at the baby as he walked her and Keisha to the door.

"What else are you going to tell her about the social contract?" he asked when he came back to the kitchen. "I think you've convinced her that it exists. And I like the way you compared it to a race course. That was clever."

"Maybe I'll tell her something about being active," I said. "That you have to be active with the social contract or you can't use it, like John Sunday, and some of Sly's friends. They reached a point where they stopped being active and let themselves be used by the system."

"If she's got that child's welfare at heart—and I think she does—then she'll be active," Elijah said. "She doesn't seem like the kind of person who is going to sit at the table and wait for the pot to boil."

"But the hardest thing she's going to have to deal with?" I asked.

"That people are going to be working against her," Elijah said.

"Who?"

"People who think they can take advantage of her," Elijah said. "People who want to use her talents, or her body, for their own purposes. Some people who just might not want her to get ahead in the world. You know, there are people like that."

"I think that's more or less where I was going," I said. "The social contract is not big on being fair. I think that every time you see that something is unfair, you feel bad and you want to give up."

"That's the time—cut up a couple of those vidalias from under the sink—that the theory of the social contract comes in handy," Elijah said. "You know the theory, how the system is supposed to work, and you don't close your eyes or your mind and walk away."

I took the vidalias from the closet under the sink, peeled them, and started to cut them up. Elijah was right about Keisha. She was an active person, and having CeCe in her life just gave her more motivation. Still, even she got discouraged once in a while.

"You want to add a side dish of cornbread to today's soup?" Elijah asked.

"Why?"

"Just to keep our interest going while you run down to me when we should start teaching children about the social contract," Elijah said. "Or do you think we shouldn't bother with it at all?"

"Can I go out and buy the cornbread and save my answer for tomorrow?" I asked.

"We're making the cornbread," Elijah said. "And yes, we can save your answer for tomorrow."

17

"So why are you all up into Keisha** and her baby?" Mom asked. Her face was tight and she was looking around the room, at the walls, at the clock, at anywhere except toward me.

"Mom, I'm not *all up into Keisha*!" I said. "Why are you saying that?"

"You came in here jumping up and down about how you had convinced her to come to the gym and work on her three-point *whatever* and how she was going to use the social contract to help her baby," Mom went on. "What do you have to do with her baby, anyway? Why isn't the father looking out for her?"

"Why are you mad because you thought I helped somebody?" I asked. "You're making it seem like—"

"Paul, you spent all summer working and talking

about this social contract and who was doing what, and the best thing you can come up with is how good Keisha is and how bad everyone else is and I don't get how you can judge one person over the next!" The kitchen light was off, and the sun coming through the curtains only illuminated half of Mom's face clearly.

"Mom, who am I judging?" I asked. "Who?"

"You were talking about those friends of Sty—or Sly—or whoever, over at his place," Mom said. "They didn't do this and they didn't do that or they should have known better. Maybe those people just made a few mistakes. They're not the only ones who have made mistakes, you know."

I finally got it.

"Mom, you're talking about my father, right?"

"I'm not talking about anybody," Mom said. "I'm just saying that you shouldn't be judging people so fast."

"Okay, so you want to know what I think about him?"

"No, I don't!"

"Do you mind me telling you?"

"I'm not interested," she said.

"I think the way our society is set up, the social contract works easily for some people," I said. "And for others, it's a lot harder. Look at Anthony. He's got it made with his going to film school. His dad's a doctor and his mom is bending over backward to ease his way. All that's cool, and it's making his life easier. With George and Sly's other friends, it was harder. And that thing with Binky and the chukka sticks shows you that it's not always fair. And I see that."

"That's really so *big* of you!"

"Okay, I'll leave it alone if you need me to," I said. "I don't need to sit here while you put me down."

"Go on!" Mom said. "I'm listening."

"Okay, for my father it was harder, and maybe he would have had to be a superhero to handle it," I said. "Maybe he realized he was up against it and it was making him sick and, like Sly said, he was self-medicating.

"One thing I know is that the social contract, no matter how you look at it, isn't going to be the same thing for everybody, and for many people, it's not going to be fair. No matter what Keisha did or didn't do, it's going to be harder on her little girl than it should be. But I know this—that if Keisha can really get into it and see how things work, she's going to be better off."

"A contract should be fair," Mom said.

"The way I see it is that it's fair for the kind of people who draw up the rules," I said. "So Rousseau and all his friends were looking at the social contract and saying that people who looked like them and who had their smarts could deal with it. The same with Locke and Hobbes and some of the others."

"I don't know any of those people," Mom said.

"You don't have to know their names," I said. "You just have to know that they were talking about how governments were set up and how the people had to live. They were talking about people who knew the rules and why they worked and were scoping them out to make sure they were getting a fair deal."

"They weren't talking about your father," Mom said. "Is that what you're saying?"

"Yes, that's it," I said. "So I know it was harder for my father and for everybody in the world who lived like he did and who didn't have the . . . the knowledge, maybe—"

"The right stuff?" Mom asked. "He didn't have the right stuff, so he was *nothing*, right?"

"He was a human being, just like the rest of us, but he had a harder way to go," I said.

"So what do you think of him?"

"Because he was a human being, I have to say he was responsible for his life," I said. "Good, bad, or indifferent, he had to be responsible for his own life."

"Even though it wasn't fair for him?"

"Yeah, even though it wasn't fair for him," I said. "But I understand him more now than I ever did. If I saw him walking down the street today, I would have a better idea of who he was than I did before. When he tried to look important, I would know why. I think that's something. And maybe it's something I can pass on to my children if I ever have any."

"You got to understanding Keisha pretty fast," Mom said.

"I had more tools to work with," I said. "I think if my father had worked with Elijah, he might have done more with his life."

"So do you think Elijah is a better man than your father?" Mom asked.

"That's not fair," I said. "You know it's not fair."

"Neither is your social contract," she said. "So

what are you saying? Is Elijah a better man than your father?"

"No, he's not," I said. "He's a different man, though. He's luckier, and the circumstances of his life are different, and that's good for him, just the way what my father ran into was bad for him. Sly is different, too. And D-Boy. We all have to deal with the life we get."

"Do you love your father?" Mom asked. "And I know that's not fair, so don't even go there."

"No, but I understand him better."

"That's not the same," Mom said.

"I know, Mom," I said. "I know."

Mom came over and stood behind my chair for a moment, and then I felt her arms go around me, and it was good. She didn't bring up Keisha anymore that night, or Elijah, or my father. It was as if she had settled something in her mind, the idea that I wouldn't go through life hating my father. I remembered what Elijah had said about that, that we learn to forgive those who have come before us. I imagined that one day, if I ever had kids, they would have to learn to forgive me.

What I thought, too, was that Hobbes, and

Rousseau, and Rawls and all those people who had written about the social contract had had little to do with people like my father. They were dealing with other thinkers and other people talking about social contract ideals in ways that were only vaguely connected to the life my father had led.

When it came down to it, Elijah and I were talking like that too. We were serving up soup and theory, but when it all came together, when the soup was right and you knew it, then it made you feel good. And when the theory was right and you could see and feel it was right, you knew that maybe—just maybe—you had a chance to make changes in the world.

In the end, for people like my father—like my dad—and like me, and Paris B and the other seniors, sometimes all we could see at the bottom of the social ladder was our struggle to get someplace we could call fair. But if we worked harder and tried harder, we wanted to lift our heads above the rest, and that was good too.

I liked John Sunday, and I even liked George, who had spent half his life in jail, and I hoped good things would happen to them, but I knew I didn't want to be the same as them. I wanted my share of fair to be what I worked for, and that wasn't how I had started off the summer. That's what I learned while I was cutting up vidalias and making stock.

What some people wanted was sometimes too hard to get, and the stress of trying was sometimes too hard to deal with. I think it was too hard for my father.

What I didn't know was why you could tell people what they needed to be doing and then just watch them sit and do nothing. Keisha was all about getting up and doing something, getting her game together and moving on, while that girl Sly had brought to lunch, Johnnie, wasn't doing much of anything. I think she was kind of overwhelmed. Maybe doing well in life was just too hard for some people. That's not what I wanted, but it was what I was coming to believe.

I didn't think that Miss Watkins's pastor was right about not everybody wanting to go to heaven. Everybody was probably down with going to heaven, but some people just weren't going to bust a move to get there.

I sometimes wonder if I could have taught my father about the social contract. I didn't think he would really ever take it from me. He wasn't comfortable with that whole father-son thing, and me teaching him would have been too hard to take. Elijah could have taught him more. Elijah with his patience and with all the thinking that man had done over the years.

Elijah made me bigger over the summer. It wasn't just having more things to think about. Now I've got more room inside my head for other people, and more understanding of what they are about even though I don't have all the answers. I know a little more about the individuals I met, Sister Effie, Paris B, John Sunday, Miss Watkins, Miss Fennell, and Sly. I really don't know much more about my father, but I think I would have listened harder if he was still around to talk to me.

Yeah, and I can make some good soup, too.

ALL THE RIGHT STUFF

A Q&A Between Walter Dean Myers
and Ross Workman, Coauthor of *Kick*

An Excerpt from *Darius & Twig*

A Q&A Between Walter Dean Myers and Ross Workman, Coauthor of *Kick*

Ross Workman: What made you decide to write a book about the social contract?
Walter Dean Myers: In talking to young men in juvenile facilities, I noticed that the things I took for granted—how to navigate through the rules and customs of society—were completely absent from their radar. I felt a need to explain that these rules and customs did, indeed, exist and were meaningful to their lives.

RW: Why did you write this book as a novel instead of as nonfiction? Did you always intend to write it as a novel?
WDM: The novel has a cultural relevance a nonfiction piece would have lacked. It gives me the opportunity to express my feelings to a particular group. The novel form also allows more latitude in bringing in different opinions about the social contract.

RW: Is soup used as a metaphor in the book?
WDM: I felt the varied ingredients in making a good soup were similar to the social contract in that both the social contract and soup have variations, but the blending of these variations still has quite sensible rules.

RW: Do you think the rules of the social contract have changed in a positive or negative way during your lifetime?

WDM: The major change seems to be the reaction to a truly secure society. The United States has become so secure, as far as basic survival goes, that many people think they can simply ignore the rules and still function nicely.

RW: Elijah tells Paul they are taking "all the right stuff" and putting it in the soup. Later Keisha says she wants to give her baby "all the right stuff." What made you use this phrase as the title?

WDM: Phoebe, my editor! I wanted to call the book *Soup*!

RW: What would you say to someone like Sly, who says that the social contract is a "bunch of rules so that some people can stay on top and be comfortable while people like you and me can learn to get comfortable on the bottom"?

WDM: Sly is correct. Of course you have to define "some people." People who work within the laws and customs of a society and therefore promote the well-being of the society as a whole will do well. Others who ignore the social contract or are ignorant of it will do less well.

RW: Do you think most people live their lives like John Sunday, not knowing there is a social contract and just living how they like, or do you think more people are like Elijah?

WDM: Unexpected question! The older I get, the more I believe that there are people like John Sunday who simply don't get it. They have a vague idea of rules, laws, etc., but elect not to do the work of seeing how to implement them in their own lives. The people who do the work, who figure it all out, are going to have fuller, more complete lives. The Elijahs of the world, on every level, will ultimately rule.

RW: Elijah used to be a history teacher. You often write about history. Are you a little like Elijah?

WDM: A compliment! I think that a good part of Elijah's "wisdom" is that he is simply old and has seen a lot. Wait a minute—are you saying I am simply old?

Ross, one of the interesting things about getting old is that you reach a point of summarizing your life. How did I get where I find myself? What has happened to my friends who have found themselves in less fortunate circumstances? Here is where you see the social contract most clearly. Simply by staying out of jail (following the rules of the judiciary) and learning to read with purpose (using the tools society has offered), I've done reasonably well in life. I've also happily abandoned the idea of ideal-state mythology in which "fair" is interpreted as equal benefit despite less-than-equal input. Why others haven't done as much is a lot clearer at seventy-four than it was at twenty-four.

RW: Keisha says that the social contract didn't work for her because of her home life. Now that she has a baby, how can Keisha get the social contract to work for her so she and her baby have a good future?
WDM: If Keisha truly becomes cognizant of the ins and outs of the social contract as it works in the United States, she can do the work of getting an education, do the work of keeping herself debt-free and out of jail, and succeed. This sounds fairly conservative but I truly believe it.

RW: What is the most important thing you would like readers to learn from *All the Right Stuff*?
WDM: That all societies formulate rules for the well-being of the state and its citizens. These rules dictate how the individual is allowed to succeed in a way that promotes the welfare of the state and does not harm his fellow citizens. An individual can try to change the rules to make them fairer or more favorable to

his own situation, but he cannot ignore them or break them with impunity. If my readers come away from this book with this knowledge they will at least understand what society expects of them.

An Excerpt from *Darius & Twig*

chapter one

High above the city, above the black tar rooftops, the dark brick chimneys spewing angry wisps of burnt fuel, there is a black speck making circles against the gray patchwork of Harlem sky. From the park below it looks like a small bird. No, it doesn't look like a small bird, but what else could it be?

At the end of a bench, a young man holds up a running shoe.

"It doesn't weigh anything."

"That's the thing," Twig said. "There's going to be nothing keeping me back except gravity. When I hit the track in these babies, I'm going to be flying!"

"The heel is flat. Why doesn't it have a heel?" I asked.

"Because this shoe doesn't want my heels touching the ground," Twig said, smiling. "This shoe doesn't play. This is eighty-five dollars' worth of kick-ass running, my man."

"You paid eighty-five dollars for these shoes?"

"Coach Day got them for me because I'm on the team."

"Looks good, I guess," I said, handing the track shoe back to Twig.

"Hey, Darius, my grandmother said you should come by this weekend," Twig said. "I told her that you were really Dominican but didn't want to admit it."

"Why did you tell her that?" I asked. "I'm not Dominican."

"Right, but she thinks she's a detective," Twig said. "When you come over, she's going to break out into some Spanish in her Dominican accent and see how you answer. She thinks you're going to come back in Spanish, and then she's got you!"

"Why do you do stuff like that?"

"Because it's fun," Twig said.

"It's stupid," I said.

"A little," Twig said, smiling. "But it's fun, too. You saw Mr. Ramey today? You said you were going to talk to him about a scholarship."

"I saw him," I said.

"Didn't go too good?" The corners of Twig's mouth tightened.

"I ran into the numbers," I said. "He asked me what my grade-point average was, as if he didn't already have it. I told him it was about three-point-two and he just shrugged and said it was closer to three even."

"You show him the letter from Miss Carroll?"

"Yeah, she already spoke to him about me," I said. "The thing I couldn't get around was that she was saying I'm smart—"

"You are, man!"

"Okay, but what he's saying is that when you send a transcript to a college, they want to see the numbers written down that say you're smart. Two-point-five isn't going to make anybody jump up and down unless you're six nine or can run a ten-second hundred yards wearing football cleats."

"Man, you got too much on the ball not to get a scholarship to some school," Twig said. "You tell him about the letter you got from that magazine?"

"How if I revise my story they might publish it?"

"Yeah."

"I showed it to him so he could see it was real," I said. "He got right to the bottom line. He said that right now I wasn't scholarship material. If the *Delta Review* actually published the story, I should come back to him and he'd call a few colleges. I don't think he thought I had a chance. The *Delta Review* is a college quarterly, Twig. It's got a lot of prestige and everybody who's a serious writer is shooting for it."

"He's a cold dude, Darius," Twig said.

"No, man, it's a cold-ass world. When you open the refrigerator and you get cold coming out, you should expect it."

"That's all he had to say?"

"No, he said that maybe I should drop out and do my junior year over again. He said he wasn't recommending it but that I should maybe think about it."

"You going to do that?"

"No. I could run into the same thing I ran into this year and then just not finish high school," I said. "This way at least I'm on the track to graduating."

"You tell him why your grades were messed up?"

"I started to get at it but he didn't want to hear it," I said. "He wasn't bitchy about it or anything like that, but he laid it out straight. He said that what I needed, a full scholarship in a school away from Harlem, just wasn't going to happen."

"So what you going to do?"

"Hope I can fix up the story so that they'll publish it," I said.

"You can do it, bro," Twig said. "I know you can do it!"

"He called up Miss Carroll when I was sitting there," I said. "He asked her point friggin' blank if I had a chance to get published. She said I had a chance, but the way she said it—"

"He had her on speakerphone?"

"Yes. The way she said it was like . . . she didn't much believe in it," I said. "She told him that they probably had hundreds of submissions and mine had to be one of the better ones if they were even considering it. She was pushing for me, but she was being realistic."

"What did Ramey have to say about that?"

"He said that the colleges wanted to know what *happened*, not what *could* have happened."

I watched as Twig laced on his new running shoes and tried them out on the track. He looked happy as he ran. I was watching him but in my head I was replaying the conversation between me and Mr. Ramey, the school's guidance counselor. He had said a lot of things about how well I had tested when I entered the school, and how much promise I had. Then he went on about my chances for a scholarship. That was the short part of the conversation. I had figured it would be.

The thing was that I needed a scholarship that would get me out of my house, away from my mom, away from the hood, and most of all, away from the crap that was going on in my head every day. Mr. Ramey was right. It didn't do any good being smart. If you were smart and if the world had been right side up, then you would be rewarded for being smart. But the way the world really worked, the way it went down especially when it came to dudes like me, was that you had to walk a path to show you were smart and it didn't have anything to do with what you had in your head or in your heart. It had to do with what you scored on tests, the grades you got, and what grades they could send to a college.

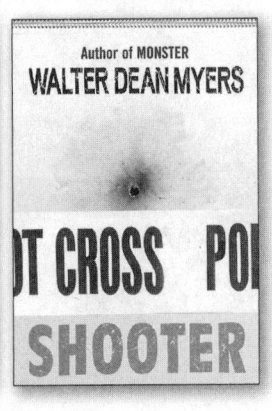